Djinn

OTHER WORKS BY ALAIN ROBBE-GRILLET
Published by Grove Press

The Erasers
For a New Novel
In the Labyrinth
Jealousy
La Maison de Rendez-Vous
Last Year at Marienbad
Project for a Revolution in New York
Topology of a Phantom City
The Voyeur

Djinn

ALAIN ROBBE-GRILLET

TRANSLATED FROM THE FRENCH BY
YVONE LENARD AND WALTER WELLS

GROVE PRESS, INC./NEW YORK

First published in French by Les Editions de Minuit, Paris, France,
1981.

First Hardcover Edition 1982
First Printing 1982
ISBN: 0-394-52569-8
Library of Congress Catalog Card Number: 81-86393

First Evergreen Edition 1982
First Printing 1982
ISBN: 0-394-17983-8
Library of Congress Catalog Card Number: 81-86393

Library of Congress Cataloging in Publication Data

Robbe-Grillet, Alain, 1922-
    Djinn.
    I. Title.
PQ2635.0117D5413   843′.914   81-86393
ISBN 0-394-52569-8   AACR2
ISBN 0-394-17983-8 (pbk.)

Manufactured in the United States of America

GROVE PRESS, INC., 196 West Houston Street, New York, N.Y. 10014

Djinn

PROLOGUE

There is nothing—I mean no incontrovertible evidence—that might allow anyone to place Simon Lecoeur's story among tales of pure fiction. In the contrary, one can observe that numerous and important elements of that unstable, incomplete text, fissured as it seems, coincide with facts (commonly known facts) with a strange recurrence that is therefore disconcerting. And, while other elements of the narrative stray deliberately away from those facts, they always do so in so suspicious a manner that one is forced to see there a systematic intent on the part of the narrator, as though some secret motive had dictated those changes and those inventions.

Such motive, of course, escapes us, at least for the time being. Were we to discover it, it would shed light on the whole affair. It is permissible, in any case, to think so.

About the author himself, little is known. His true identity is itself open to question. Nobody knew any of his relatives, distant or close. After his disappearance, a French passport was found at his home, in the name of Boris Koershimen, an electronics engineer, born in Kiev. But the police in charge of the investigation claim that document to be a crude fake, probably manufactured abroad. Yet, the photograph it bears, according to all witnesses, seems indeed to be that of the young man.

As for the officially listed last name, it hardly sounds Ukrainian. Besides, it is under a different spelling and a different first name that he had been employed at the American School of the rue de Passy,* where, for the last few months, he had been teaching contemporary literary French: "Robin Körsimos, known as Simon Lecoeur." The name would seem to indicate, this time, rather a Hungarian, or a Finn, perhaps yet even a Greek; but this last guess would be given the lie by the looks of that tall and

* The Franco-American School in Paris (E.F.A.P.) 56, rue de Passy 75016 Paris

8

slender young man, with light blond hair and pale green eyes. Finally, one must note that his colleagues at school, as well as his students (girls for the most part) called him only "Yann," which they spelled Ján when they wrote him brief memos; none of them could ever say why.

The text that concerns us—ninety-nine pages, typed double spaced—had been prominently placed on his desk (in the modest furnished room he rented at 21, rue d'Amsterdam), next to an ancient typewriter, which, according to experts, was indeed the one on which it had been typed. Yet, the date on that typescript was several weeks, probably even several months, old; and there again, the proximity of the typewriter to the papers could have been the product of some staging, a falsification invented by that elusive character in order to cover his tracks.

Reading that narrative, your first impression is that you are dealing with material for a textbook, meant for the teaching of language, such as there must be hundreds. The regular progression of the grammatical difficulties of the language appears clearly, in the course of eight chapters of increasing length, which would roughly correspond to the eight* weeks of an American university quarter.

Nevertheless, the story told in these pages remains quite far removed from the resolutely innocuous texts generally found in works of that type. As a matter of fact, the ratio of probability of the reported

* There are actually ten weeks in a quarter (Translator's note).

events is almost always too low, in relation to the laws of traditional realism. Thus, it is not ruled out to see a mere guise in this pretense of a pedagogical intent. Behind that guise, something else must be concealed. But what?

Here, in its entirety, is the text in question. At the top of the page appears this simple title: *The Rendez-vous*.

CHAPTER ONE

I arrive exactly at the appointed hour: it is six-thirty. It is almost dark already. The hangar is not locked. I walk in, pushing the door, which no longer has a lock.

Inside, all is silent. Listening more attentively, the straining ear registers only a faint sound, clear and steady, fairly close by: water dripping from some loose faucet, into a tank, a basin, or just a puddle on the ground.

Under the dim light that filters through the large

windows with dirt encrusted, partly broken panes, I can barely make out the objects that surround me, piled on all sides in great disarray, no doubt cast off: ancient discarded machinery, metallic carcasses, and assorted old hardware, which dust and rust darken to a blackish and uniformly dull tint.

When my eyes become somewhat accustomed to the semidarkness, I finally notice the man, facing me. Standing, motionless, both hands in the pockets of his trench coat, he watches me without saying a word, without so much as the slightest greeting in my direction. The character is wearing dark glasses, and the thought crosses my mind: he is perhaps blind. . . .

Tall and slender, young by all appearances, he leans a casual shoulder against a pile of oddly shaped crates. His face is not quite visible, because of the glasses, between the turned-up collar of the trench coat and the brim of the hat pulled down over his forehead. The whole figure brings irresistibly to mind some old detective movie of the thirties.

Having now myself stopped five or six steps away from the man who remains as motionless as a bronze statue, I enunciate clearly (but in a low voice) the coded message of recognition: "Monsieur Jean, I presume? My name is Boris. I come about the ad."

And all I hear again is the steady dripping of water in the silence. Is that blind man a deaf mute as well?

After several minutes, the answer finally comes: "Do not pronounce it *Jean*, but Djinn. I am an American."

My surprise is so great that I can barely hide it. The voice is, indeed, that of a young woman: lilting and warm, with husky undertones that give it a hint of senuous intimacy; yet, she does not correct the title *Monsieur*, which she therefore seems to accept.

A half smile plays upon her lips. She asks: "It bothers you to work for a girl?"

There is a challenge in the tone of her words. But I promptly decide to play the game: "No, sir," I say, "on the contrary." In any case, I have no choice.

Djinn does not seem in a hurry to speak any more. She is watching me carefully and without kindness. She is, perhaps, forming an unfavorable judgment of my abilities. I dread the verdict, which falls at the end of her examination: "You are a rather good-looking guy," she says, "but you are too tall for a Frenchman."

I feel like laughing. This young foreigner hasn't been in France long, I guess, and she has come with ready-made ideas. "I am French," I say by way of justification. "That is not the question," she answers after a silence.

She speaks French with a slight accent, which carries a lot of charm. Her lilting voice and her androgynous looks evoke, for me, the actress Jane Frank. I love Jane Frank. I go to see every single one of her movies. Unfortunately, as "Monsieur" Djinn says, that is not the question.

We remain that way, watching each other, for a few minutes more. But it is getting darker and darker. To hide my embarrassment, I ask: "So, what is the question?"

Relaxing for the first time, or so it seems, Djinn smiles the delightful smile of Jane. "You are going to have to pass unnoticed in the crowd," she says.

I am very much tempted to return her smile, accompanied by a compliment on her looks. I don't dare: she is the boss. I fall back on apologies: "I am not a giant." As a matter of fact, I am barely six one, and she herself is not short.

She wants me to move forward. I take five steps toward her. At closer range, her face has a strange pallor, a waxen immobility. I am almost afraid to move closer. I stare at her mouth. . . .

"Closer," she says. This time, there is no doubt: her lips do not move when she speaks. I take one more step and I place my hand on her chest.

This is not a woman, nor a man. What I have in front of me is a plastic mannequin for display windows. The dim light explains my mistake. The lovely smile of Jane Frank must be credited to my imagination alone.

"Touch again, if you like," says the seductive voice of Monsieur Djinn ironically, underlining the ridiculousness of my situation. Where does that voice come from? The sounds do not issue from the mannequin itself, most likely, but from a loudspeaker hidden nearby.

So, I am being watched by someone invisible. This is most unpleasant. It makes me feel clumsy, threatened, guilty. The girl who is talking to me probably happens to be sitting several miles away; and she is watching me, as though I were some bug caught in a trap, on her television screen. I am sure she is making fun of me.

"At the end of the center aisle," says the voice, "there are some stairs. Walk up to the second floor. The steps do not go any farther." Happy to part company with my lifeless doll, I am relieved to carry out these instructions.

Arriving at the first floor, I see the stairs stop there. This is therefore a second floor American style. This confirms my opinion: Djinn does not reside in France.

I am now in some sort of a vast attic, which quite resembles the ground floor: same dirty panes, and same arrangement of aisles between piles of assorted junk. There is only a little more light.

I glance left and right, seeking a human presence in this mess of cardboard, wood and iron.

Suddenly, I have the disturbing feeling that a scene is being repeated, as in a mirror: facing me, five or six steps away, stands the same motionless figure, in a trench coat with turned-up collar, dark glasses and felt hat with a turned-down brim, that is to say a second mannequin, the exact reproduction of the first, in an identical posture.

I approach, this time without hesitation; and I reach forward. . . . Fortunately, I stop my gesture in time: the thing has just smiled, and this time, beyond

any doubt, unless I am crazy. This fake wax mannequin is a real woman.

She withdraws her hand from her pocket, and
very slowly, she raises her arm to push away mine,
which remains half raised, paralyzed by surprise.

"Don't touch, boy," she says, "danger zone!" The
voice is the same indeed, with the same sensuous
allure, and the same Boston accent; except that, from
now on, she speaks to me with patronizing im-
pertinence.

"Sorry, baby," I say, "I am an idiot." In the same
severe and final tone, she replies: "According to reg-
ulations, *you* must always speak to me courteously."

"Okay," I say, without abandoning my apparent
good humor. Yet, all this staginess is beginning to get
on my nerves. Djinn is probably acting that way on
purpose, because she adds, after a moment's reflection: "And don't say *okay*, that's very vulgar, especially in French."

I am anxious to terminate this unpleasant interview: I have nothing to hope for, after such a
welcome. Yet, at the same time, this insolent girl fas-
cinates me in some disconcerting way. "Thank you,"
I say, "I appreciate the language lessons."

As though she had guessed my thoughts, she adds
then: "Impossible for you to leave us. It is too late,
the exit is guarded. Meet Laura, she is armed."

I turn around, toward the stairs. Another girl,
wearing exactly the same costume, with dark glasses
and slouch brim hat is there, at the top of the stairs,

hands pushed deep into the pockets of her raincoat.

The position of her right arm and the bulge in her pocket give some likelihood to the threat: that young lady is aiming a heavy-gauge revolver at me, hidden by the fabric. . . . Or else, she is pretending to.

"Hello, Laura, how are you?" I say in my coolest thriller-diller style. "How are you," she affirms in an echo, Anglo-Saxon style. She must be without rank in the organization, since she speaks that politely.

An absurd thought crosses my mind: Laura is nothing but the inanimate mannequin from the ground floor, who, having climbed the steps behind me, faces me again.

To tell the truth, girls are no longer the way they used to be. They play gangsters, nowadays, just like boys. They organize rackets. They plan holdups and practice karate. They will rape defenseless adolescents. They wear pants. . . . Life has become impossible.

Djinn probably feels that explanations are in order, for she breaks, at this point, into a longer speech: "I hope that you'll forgive our methods. We absolutely have to work this way: keep on the lookout for possible enemies, and watch over the loyalty of our new friends: in short, we must operate with the greatest precautions, as you have just seen."

Then, after a pause, she goes on: "Our action is secret, by necessity. It carries major risks for us. You are going to help us. We will give you precise instructions. But we prefer (at least at first) not to reveal to you the exact purpose of your mission nor the general goal of our undertaking. That is for reasons of security, but also of efficiency."

I ask her what will happen should I refuse. But she leaves me no choice: "You need money, we pay. Therefore, you accept without an argument. It is useless to ask questions or to make comments. You do what we ask of you, and that's all there is to it."

I like my freedom. I like to feel responsible for my own actions. I like to understand what I am doing. . . . And, yet, I agree to this weird deal.

It is not the fear of that imaginary gun that motivates me, nor such a great need for money. . . . There are many other ways to earn a living, when you are young. Why, then? Curiosity? Bravado? Or a more obscure motivation?

In any case, if I am free, I have the right to do what I feel like doing, even against my own good sense.

"You've got something on your mind that you are not telling," says Djinn. "Yes," I say. "And what is it?" "It has nothing to do with the job."

Djinn then removes her dark glasses, allowing me to gaze upon her lovely pale eyes. And finally, she smiles at me, the enchanting smile I have been hoping for all along, and giving up the superior tone of her position, she whispers in her warm and sweet voice: "Now, you tell me what's on your mind."

"The struggle of the sexes," I say, "is the motor of history."

18

CHAPTER TWO

Alone again, walking briskly along the streets, now brightly lit by streetlights and shop windows, I find that my mood has radically changed: a brand new exhilaration quickens my body, churns my thoughts, colors every little thing around me. It is no longer the mindless indifference of this morning, but a sort of happiness, and even enthusiasm, without precise cause. . . .

Without cause, indeed? Why not admit it? My

meeting with Djinn is the obvious cause of this sudden and remarkable transformation. At every moment, for any reason or for no reason at all, I think of her. Her image, her silhouette, her face, her gestures, the way she moves, above all her smile are much too present in my mind; my job certainly does not require that I pay that much attention to the person of my employer.

I look at the shops (rather unattractive in this part of town), the passersby, the dogs (usually I hate dogs), with benevolence. I want to sing, to run. I see smiles on every face. Ordinarily, people look dumb and sad. Today, they have been touched by some inexplicable grace.

My new job is certainly fun: it has the taste of adventure. But it has more than that: It has the taste of an adventure that is a love affair. . . . I have always been a romantic, and fond of make-believe, that's for certain. I should, therefore, be doubly careful in this matter. My runaway imagination might well cause errors in my judgments and even gross mistakes in my actions.

Suddenly, a forgotten detail surfaces in my memory: I am supposed to pass unnoticed. Djinn said so, and she insisted on it several times. Well, I happen to be doing exactly the contrary: no doubt everyone notices my joyful euphoria, and this thought calms me down considerably.

I walk into a café, and I order a black espresso. The French like only Italian coffee; "French" coffee is

20

not strong enough. But worst of all, for them, is American coffee. . . . Why am I thinking of America? Because of Djinn, once more! This is beginning to get to me.

A paradox: in order not to be noticed, in France, one asks for an Italian espresso. Is there such a thing, as "the French," or "the Americans"? The French are like this. . . . The French eat this, and not that. . . . The French dress this way, they walk that way. . . . Where eating is concerned, yes, it might still be true, but less and less. A sign above the counter lists foods and prices; I read: hot dog, pizza, sandwiches, rollmops, merguez. . . .

The waiter brings a small cup of very black liquid, which he places on the table in front of me, with two cubes of sugar wrapped together in white paper. Then, he walks away, picking up on his way a used glass left on another table.

I realize then that I am not the only customer in this bistro which was, however, empty when I came in. I have company, a young woman sitting nearby, a student apparently, wearing a red jacket and engrossed in a heavy medical textbook.

While I observe her, she seems to sense my stare, and raises her eye in my direction. I think ironically: now, I've done it, I've really struck out, I've been noticed. She gazes at me silently, at length, as though not seeing me. Then she returns her attention to her book.

But, a few seconds later, she examines me again,

and this time she says in a neutral voice, with a sort of quiet assurance: "It's five past seven. You are going to be late." She hasn't even looked at her watch. I check mine automatically. It is indeed five past seven. And I do have an appointment at quarter past seven at the Gare du Nord.

So, this girl is a spy, staked out by Djinn on my path to check my professional dedication. "You work with us?" I say after a moment's reflection. Then, since she does not answer, I ask further: "How come you know so much about me? You know who I am, where I am going, what I have to do, and at what time. You're a friend of Djinn, then?"

She looks me over with cold interest, also no doubt with disapproval, because she finally states flatly: "You talk too much." And she turns her attention back to her work. Thirty seconds later, without raising an eye, she pronounces a few words, slowly, as though speaking to herself. She seems to be deciphering a difficult passage of her book: "The street you are looking for is the third on the right, straight down the avenue."

To tell the truth, this guardian angel is right: If I hang around here arguing, I'm going to be late. "I thank you," I say, showing my independence by an overly formal bow. I rise, I go to the counter, I pay for my coffee and I push the door.

Once outside, I glance backward toward the large, brightly lit room empty but for the girl in the red jacket. She is no longer reading. She has closed her heavy book on her table, and she follows me with her eyes, showing no embarrassment, with a hard and steady expression.

In spite of my desire to do just the contrary, to assert my freedom, I continue walking in the right direction, on the avenue, among the crowd of men and women returning home from work. They are no longer carefree and attractive. From now on, I am convinced they are all watching me. At the third intersection, I turn right into a dark and deserted, narrow street.

Devoid of any automobile traffic, even of parked cars, and lit here and there only by a few old-fashioned street lamps that cast a yellow flickering light, abandoned—so it seems—by its very inhabitants, this infrequented side street contrasts completely with the major thoroughfare I have just left. The houses are low (two stories at most) and poor, no lights in the windows. Anyway, it's mostly hangars and workshops here. The ground is uneven, cobbled in the old style, in very bad condition, with puddles of dirty water where the paving stones are missing.

I hesitate to venture farther into this long and narrow passage, which looks very much like a dead end: in spite of the darkness, I can make out a blind wall that appears to block the far end. Yet, a blue enamel plaque at the entrance bore the name of a real street; I mean one passable at both ends: "Rue Vercingétorix III." I wasn't aware of the existence of a third Vercingétorix, or even a second. . . .

Reflecting, I thought there might, indeed, be a passage at the far end, to the right or the left. But the total absence of automobile traffic is disquieting. Am I really on the right track? My thought was to take the next street, with which I am familiar. I am certain that it leads to the railway station almost as quickly. Only the intervention of the medical student has sent me on this so-called shortcut.

Time is short. My appointment at the railway station is, by now, less than five minutes away. This Godforsaken alley might mean a worthwhile saving of time. It is in any case, good for going fast: no vehicles or pedestrians impeding progress and no crossing either.

Having accepted the risk (somewhat at random, unfortunately), I must, in the absence of a sidewalk, place my feet carefully where the ground is even . . . taking the longest possible strides. I'm going so fast I have the feeling I'm flying, as in a dream.

I am ignorant, for the time being, of the exact meaning of my mission: it consists only in spotting a certain traveler (whose precise description I have memorized) arriving on the train from Amsterdam at 7:12 P.M. Next, I am discreetly to tail the character all the way to his hotel. That's it for now. I hope to learn the rest soon.

I haven't yet gone halfway down this endless street, when suddenly a child bursts across ten yards in front of me. He comes from one of the houses on the right, one a little taller than its neighbors, and he

24

runs across the street as fast as his little legs will carry him.

On the run, he trips over an uneven paving stone and falls into a puddle of blackish mud without a cry. He lies still, sprawled with his arms thrown out in front of him.

A few quick strides and I am bending over the motionless little body. I turn him over carefully. He is a boy, about ten years old, dressed strangely: like a kid from the last century, with breeches, knee socks, and a full smock, rather short, cinched at the waist by a wide leather belt.

His eyes are wide open: but his pupils are fixed. His mouth isn't closed, his lips tremble slightly. His limbs are limp and inert, as well as his neck; his entire body is like a rag doll.

Luckily, he did not fall into the mud, but just on the edge of that hole full of dirty water. This water, looked at more closely, seems viscous, brown, almost red rather than black. A strange anxiety suddenly overwhelms me. Does the color of this unknown liquid scare me? Or what else?

I check my watch. It is 7:09. Impossible, now, to be at the railway station in time for the train from Amsterdam. My whole adventure, born just this morning, is already over, then. But I can't find it within me to abandon this injured child, even for the love of Djinn. . . . Oh well! Anyway, I've missed the train.

A door on my right is wide open. The boy undoubtedly comes from that house. Yet, there is no light that I can see inside, neither at the ground floor, nor the one above. I lift the boy's body in my arms. It is extremely thin, light as a bird.

Under the faint glow of the streetlight nearby, I get a better look at his face: he has no apparent injury, he is calm and handsome, but exceedingly pale. His skull must have hit a paving stone, and he is still unconscious from the impact. Yet, he has fallen forward, arms outstretched. His head did not, therefore, hit the ground.

I pass over the threshold of the house, the frail burden draped over my arms. I proceed with caution, down the long corridor that runs perpendicular to the street. All is dark and silent.

Having found no other way to go—no door or cross hall—I come upon a wooden staircase. I seem to glimpse a faint light from the floor above. I walk up slowly, for I'm afraid of stumbling or hitting some invisible obstacle with the legs or the head of the still-unconscious kid.

Two doors open onto the landing of the second floor. One is closed, the other slightly ajar. This is where the faint light comes from. I push the door with my knee and enter a room of very large dimensions, with two windows looking out onto the street.

There is no light in the room. There is only the glow of the streetlights that comes from outside through the curtainless windowpanes. It allows me to make out the shapes of the furniture: a bare wooden table, three or four unmatched chairs, their seats more or less caved in, an iron bedstead and a large number of trunks of various shapes and sizes.

The bedstead holds a mattress, but no sheets or blankets. I place the child, with all possible care, onto this crude couch. He is still unconscious, with no sign of life except for a very faint breathing. His pulse is almost imperceptible. But his large eyes, remaining open, shine in the gloomy light.

I glance around for an electric switch or something else that might provide light. But I see nothing of the kind. I notice, at this point, that there isn't a single light—chandelier, shaded lamp or bare bulb—in the entire room.

I step back out on the landing and I call out, in a low voice at first, then louder. No answer whatsoever reaches my ears. The whole house is plunged into total silence, as though abandoned. I don't know what else to do. I am abandoned myself, outside of time.

Then, a sudden thought takes me back to the windows of the room: Where was the kid going on his brief run? He was crossing the road from one side to the other, straightaway. He might, therefore, live on the other side.

But, on the other side of the street there are no houses: only a long brick wall with no apparent opening at all. A little farther on the left there is a fence in disrepair. I go back to the stairs and I call out again, still in vain. I listen to the pounding of my own heart. I have a very strong feeling, now, that time has stopped.

A faint creaking sound, in the room, calls me back to my patient. Two steps away from the bed I am jolted, instinctively recoiling. The boy is in exactly the same position as before, but now he has a large crucifix laid on his chest, a dark wooden cross with a silver Christ, that reaches from shoulder to waist.

I glance all around. There is no one but the child lying outstretched. So my first thought is that he himself is responsible for this macabre setting: he pretends to have fainted, but he moves when my back is turned. I examine his face very closely; his features are as frozen as those of a wax figure, and his complexion just as pallid. He looks like an effigy sculpted upon a tomb.

At that moment, looking up, I become aware of the presence of a second child, standing at the threshold of the room; a little girl of about seven or eight, motionless in the doorway. Her eyes are fixed upon me.

Where does she come from? How did she get here? No sound has signaled her approach. In the dim light, I clearly distinguish, nevertheless, her white, old-fashioned dress with fitted bodice and wide gathered skirt, full but rather stiff, falling all the way to her ankles.

"Hello," I say, "is your mama here?"

The girl keeps staring at me silently. The whole scene is so unreal, ghostly, frozen, that the sound of my own voice rings strangely off-key to me, unlikely, as it were, in this spellbound atmosphere under the weird bluish light. . . .

As there is nothing else to do but venture a few words, I force myself to speak this innocuous sentence:

"Your brother fell."

My syllables fall, too, awakening neither response nor echo, like useless objects deprived of sense. And silence closes in again. Have I really spoken? Cold, numbness, paralysis begin to spread through my limbs.

CHAPTER THREE

How long did the spell last?
Suddenly making up her mind, the little girl walks decisively toward me without a word. I make an immense effort to pull out of my pervading numbness. I rub my hand over my forehead, over my eyelids, again and again. I finally manage to come back up to the surface. Little by little, I am regaining my senses.

To my great surprise, I am now seated on a straw

chair at the head of the bed. By my side, the boy is still asleep, lying on his back, his eyes open, the crucifix on his chest. I manage to stand without too much effort.

The little girl holds before her a brass candelabrum which shines like gold; it is fitted with three unlit candles. She walks without the slightest sound, gliding in the manner of an apparition, but that is because of her felt-sole slippers.

She places the candelabrum on the chair I have just left. Then she lights the three candles, one after another, with care, each time lighting a new match and blowing out the flame after use, to return the blackened stub to the box afterward with total concentration.

I ask: "Where is there a telephone? We are going to call a doctor for your brother."

The little girl watches me with a kind of condescension, as one does when addressed by a maniac or a half-wit.

"Jean is not my brother," she says. "And the doctor is of no use, since Jean is dead."

She speaks in the conciliatory tone of a grown-up, not at all like a child. Her voice is well modulated and sweet, but expresses no emotion. Her features very much resemble those of the unconscious boy, in a more feminine way of course.

"His name is Jean?" I say. The question is superfluous; but suddenly the memory of Djinn overwhelms me and I feel, once more, a violent despair. It

31

is now past seven-thirty. The affair is pretty well finished, I should say pretty badly finished. . . . The little girl shrugs her shoulders:

"Obviously," she says. "What do you want to call him?" Then, still with the same grave and reasonable air, she goes on: "Already, yesterday, he died."

"What are you talking about? When one dies, it's forever."

"No, not Jean!" she states with such categorical certainty that I myself feel shaken. I smile inwardly, nevertheless, at the idea of the bizarre spectacle that she and I are making, and of the absurd dialogue we are exchanging. But I choose to play the game.

"He dies often?"

"These days, yes, rather often. Other times, he will go several days without dying."

"And it lasts long?"

"An hour perhaps, or a minute, or a century. I do not know. I do not have a watch."

"He comes out of death by himself? Or you must help him?"

"Sometimes he comes back by himself. Generally, it's when I wash his face; you know: the last rites."

I am beginning to grasp, now, the likely meaning of this whole scene: the boy must have frequent fainting spells, probably of nervous origin; cold water on his brow serves to revive him. I cannot, however, leave these children alone until the boy regains consciousness.

The candle flame now casts a pink glow on his face. Warmer highlights soften the shadows around his mouth and his nose. His pupils, under this new glow, reflect dancing lights, breaking the fixed stare of his eyes.

The little girl in the white dress sits down carelessly on the bed, at the feet of the would-be corpse. I can't refrain from reaching out, to protect the boy from her jolting the metal box spring. I get, in return, a scornful glare.

"The dead do not feel anything. You should know that. They are not even here. They sleep in another world, with their dreams. . . ." Lower, more confidential tones muffle the timbre of her voice, which grows softer and more faraway to whisper: "Often, I sleep next to him, when he is dead; we leave together for heaven."

A feeling of void, an immeasurable anguish, once more, assaults my mind. Neither my good will nor my presence serve any purpose. I want to leave this haunted room; it weakens my body and my reason. If I can manage to get a satisfactory explanation, I will leave immediately. I repeat my first question:

"Where is your mama?"

"She is gone."

"When is she coming back?"

"She is not coming back," says the little girl.

I no longer dare to insist any further. I sense here some family drama, painful and secret. I say, to change the subject:

"And your papa?"

"He died."

"How many times?"

The stare of her eyes, widened by surprise, full of pity and reproach, soon make me feel guilty. After a remarkably long time, she finally condescends to explain:

"You are talking nonsense. When people die, it is final. Even children know that." Which is logic itself, by all evidence.

I am not getting anywhere. How can these kids live here alone, all by themselves, without father or mother? Perhaps they live elsewhere, with grand-parents or friends, who have taken them in as an act of charity. But, more or less left to themselves, they wander all day here and there. And this empty, run-down building, without electricity or telephone, is only their favorite playground. I ask:

"Where do you live, you and your brother?"

"Jean is not my brother," she says. "He is my husband."

"And you live with him in this house?"

"We live where we want to. And if you don't like our house, why did you come? We didn't ask anything of anyone."

After all, she is right. I have no idea myself what I am doing here. I sum up the situation in my head: a phony medical student redirects me into an alley I did not choose; I see a kid run just in front of me; he falls and faints dead away; I carry his body to the nearest shelter; there, a grown-up sounding and mys-tical little girl holds forth without rhyme or reason on the subject of the absent and the dead.

"If you want to see his portrait, it's hanging on the wall," she says by way of conclusion. How did she guess I was still thinking of her father?

On the wall she points to, between the two windows, a small ebony frame does hold the photograph of a man, about thirty, in the uniform of a petty officer. A commemorative sprig of boxwood has been slipped under the black wood of the frame.

"He was a sailor?"

"Obviously."

"He died at sea?"

I am sure she is going to say "Obviously" again, with that barely perceptible shrug of the shoulders. But, in fact, her answers always disappoint my expectations. And, this time, she only rectifies it, like a teacher correcting a pupil: "Lost at sea," which is the accurate expression when speaking of a shipwreck.

Yet, such distinctions are hardly what one would expect coming from a child that age. And I suddenly feel that she is mouthing a well-rehearsed lesson. Under the photograph, a careful hand has written these words: "For Marie and Jean, their loving Papa." I half turn to the little girl:

"You are called Marie?"

"Obviously. What else do you want to call me?"

While I examine the portrait, I can suddenly sense a trap. But already the little girl goes on:

"And you, you are called Simon. There is a letter for you, Si."

I have just noticed a white envelope protruding

slightly from under the sprig of boxwood. So I don't have time to mull over the surprising changes in Marie's behavior: now, she knows my first name and uses it as though she knew me well.

I carefully grasp the letter with two fingers, and I pull it out of its hiding place without damaging the leaves of the boxwood. Light and air will soon turn this kind of paper yellow. Yet, it is neither yellowed, nor old, as far as I can tell under this poor light. It can't have been here long.

The envelope bears the complete name of the addressee: "Monsieur Simon Lecoeur, alias Boris"— that is to say, not only my own name, but also the password of the organization for which I have been working barely a few hours.

More strangely yet, the writing resembles in every way (same ink, same pen, same hand) that on the dedication of the sailor's photograph. . . .

But, at this very moment, the little girl shouts at the top of her lungs, behind me: "All right, Jean, you may wake up. He has found the message."

I turn with a start, and I see the inanimate kid sit up suddenly on the edge of the mattress, legs dangling, next to his delighted sister. Both of them applaud in unison and shake with mirth as the metal box spring vibrates under their laughter for almost a minute. I feel like a complete idiot.

Then Marie, as abruptly as before, turns serious again. The boy soon does likewise; he obeys—I think—this little girl who is clearly younger than he, but sharper. She declares then for my benefit:

36

"Now, it is you who are our papa. I am Marie Lecoeur. And this is Jean Lecoeur."

She leaps to her feet to point to her accomplice, ceremoniously, while taking a bow in my direction. Next, she runs to the door that opens onto the landing; there, she apparently presses an electric switch (placed outside), for suddenly a brilliant light fills the entire room, as in a theater at intermission.

The many lamps, antique sconces shaped like birds, are as a matter of fact quite visible; but when unlit, they can well pass unnoticed. Marie, quick and light, has come back to the bed where she sat again close to her big brother. They whisper in each other's ear.

Then, they stare at me again. They now have a quiet and attentive look. They want to see what comes next. They are at the theater, and I am on the stage, performing an unknown play, written for me by a man I do not know . . . or perhaps a woman?

I open the unsealed envelope. In it, there is a sheet of paper, folded in four. I unfold it carefully. The handwriting is still the same, that of a left handed man, no doubt, or, more accurately, of a left handed woman. My heart leaps when I see the signature. . . .

Not only that, but I can suddenly understand better my instinctive suspicion, of a moment ago, at the sight of the letters slanting backward, under the black framed portrait: very few people, in France, write with their left hand, especially in that sailor's generation.

The letter is hardly a love letter, undoubtedly. But a few words mean a lot, especially when they come from someone whom one has just lost forever. In high spirits now, facing my youthful audience, I read the text aloud, like a comedian:

"The Amsterdam train was a false track, meant to mislead suspicions. The true mission begins here. Now that you have met, the children will lead you where you are supposed to go together. Good luck."

The letter is signed "Jean," that is to say Djinn, without any possible error. But I don't get the part about suspicions. Who's supposed to be suspicious? I refold the paper, and I slip it back into its envelope. Marie applauds briefly. Jean imitates her, with some delay, unenthusiastically.

"I'm hungry," he says. "I get tired being dead."

The two children then come toward me, and each grabs one of my hands, with authority. I let them, since these are the instructions. Thus we leave, the three of us, going first out of the room, then out of the house, like a family on an outing.

The staircase and the downstairs hall, like the upstairs landing, are now also brilliantly lit by power-ful bulbs. (Who in the world has turned them on?) Since Marie, as we leave, doesn't turn off the lights or close the door, I ask her why. Her answer is no more surprising than the rest of the situation:

"It doesn't matter," she says, "since Jeanne and Joseph are here."

"Who are Jeanne and Joseph?"

"Well, Joseph is Joseph and Jeanne is Jeanne . . ."

I complete her sentence myself: ". . . obviously."

She pulls me by the hand toward the large avenue, walking with a quick step, or sometimes hopping, hopscotch fashion, on the uneven paving stones. Jean, on the contrary, lets himself be dragged along. After a few minutes, he repeats:

"I am very hungry."

"It is time for his dinner," says Marie. "He's got to be fed. Otherwise he is going to die again; and we haven't got the time anymore to play that game."

Saying these last words, she bursts into a short, shrill laugh that doesn't sound right. She is quite mad, like most children who are too grown-up for their age. I wonder how old she could be, in fact. She is short and petite, but she might be a lot older than eight.

"Marie, how old are you?"

"It's bad manners, you know, to question ladies on the subject of their age."

"Even at this age?"

"Obviously. There is no age to learn manners."

She delivered this pronouncement in a sententious tone, without the slightest smile of connivance. Is she or is she not conscious of the absurdity of her reasoning? She has turned to the left, onto the avenue, pulling us both, Jean and me, after her. Her step, as decisive as her character, does not encourage questions. But she suddenly stops short to ask one herself, staring up at me sternly:

"What about you? Do you know how to lie?"

"Sometimes, when it's necessary."

"I can lie very well, even when it's pointless. When one lies out of necessity, it has less value, obviously. I can go for a whole day without saying a single true thing. I even won a lying award, at school, last year."

"You are lying," I say. But my reply doesn't bother her for a second. She goes on, brooking no interruption, with quiet self-assurance:

"In our Logic class this year, we are doing lying exercises of the second degree. We are also studying first-degree lying with two unknowns. And sometimes, we lie in harmony. It's very exciting. In the advanced class, the girls do second-degree lying, with two unknowns, and lying of the third degree. That must be hard. I can't wait till next year."

Then, just as suddenly, she springs forward again. As for the boy, he doesn't open his mouth. I ask:

"Where are we going?"

"To the restaurant."

"We have time?"

"Obviously. What was written in the letter?"

"That you are going to take me where I'm supposed to go."

"Then, since I am taking you to the restaurant, you must therefore go to the restaurant."

That is indeed logic itself. Anyway, we arrive in front of a coffee shop. The little girl pushes the glass door with authority, and surprising vigor. We walk in behind her, Jean and I. I immediately recognize the café where I met the medical student in the red jacket. . . .

She is still there, sitting at the same place, in the center of the large empty room. She stands up when she sees us enter. I am convinced that she has been watching for my return. Passing close to us, she gives Marie a little sign and says in a low voice:

"Everything's okay?"

"Fine," says Marie, very loud and unconcerned. And she adds immediately: "Obviously."

The phony student leaves, not favoring me with a glance. We sit at one of the rectangular tables in the back of the room. For no apparent reason, the children choose the least-lighted one. They seem to avoid overly bright lights. In any case, it is up to Marie to decide.

"I want a pizza," says Jean.

"No," says his sister, "you know very well they stuff them with bacteria and viruses, on purpose."

Well, I say to myself, prophylaxy is gaining ground among the young generation. Or else, are these kids raised by an American family? As the waiter approaches, Marie orders *croque-monsieur* for everyone, two 7-Ups, "and a beer for Monsieur, who is a Russian." She makes an awful face at me, while the man walks away, still silent.

"Why did you say I was Russian? Anyway, Russians don't drink any more beer than the French, or the Germans . . ."

"You are a Russian, because your name is Boris. And you drink beer like everybody else, Boris Lecoeurovich!"

Then changing both her tone and her subject, she leans toward my ear to whisper in a confidential tone:

"Did you notice the face on that waiter? That's him in the photograph, in the sailor's uniform, in the mourning frame."

"He is really dead?"

"Obviously. Lost at sea. His ghost comes back to serve in the café where he used to work in days gone by. That's why he never says a word."

"Ah well," I say. "I see."

The man in the white jacket appears suddenly in front of us with the drinks. His resemblance to the sailor is not obvious. Marie tells him, acting very worldly:

"I do thank you. My mother will come around tomorrow to pay the bill."

CHAPTER FOUR

While we were eating, I asked Marie how that waiter could be employed in a café before his death, since he was a sailor. But that did not cause her to lose her poise:

"That was obviously during his shore leaves. As soon as he hit shore, he would come to see his mistress, who worked here. And he would serve with her, out of love, glasses of white wine and cups of coffee. Love, it makes one do great things."

"What about his mistress? What became of her?"

"When she heard of her lover's tragic end, she committed suicide, by eating a mass-produced pizza."

Next, Marie wanted me to tell her how people live in Moscow, since she had just granted me Russian citizenship. I told her that she ought to know, since she was my daughter. She then made up another cock-and-bull story:

"Oh, but no. We did not live with you. Gypsies had kidnapped us, Jean and me, when we were just babies. We lived in caravans, crisscrossed Europe and Asia, begged, sang, danced in circuses. Our adoptive parents even forced us to steal money, or things from stores.

"When we disobeyed, they would punish us cruelly: Jean had to sleep on the flying trapeze, and I in the tiger's cage. Fortunately, the tiger was quite nice; but he had nightmares and he would roar all night long. This would wake me up with a start. When I got up in the morning, I had never had enough sleep.

"You, in the meantime, were searching the world for us. You would go every night to the circus—a new circus every night—and you would roam backstage to question all the little children you found. But I bet you were mostly looking at the pretty bareback riders. . . . So it is only today that we found each other again."

Marie was speaking fast, with a sort of anxious certainty. Suddenly, her excitement fell. She thought for a moment in a sudden dreamy mood, then she concluded sadly:

"And still, we're not certain that we have found each other. Perhaps it is not us, nor you, either. . . ."

Probably judging that she had spoken enough nonsense, Marie next declared that it was my turn to tell a story.

Since I ate faster than the children, I have finished my croque-monsieur some time ago. Marie, who chews every mouthful slowly and carefully in between her lengthy speeches, doesn't seem anywhere near having finished her meal. I want to know what kind of a story she wishes to hear. She says—that's definite—"a story of love and science fiction." So I begin:

"Here you go. A robot meets a young lady. . . ."

My listener allows me to go no further.

"You don't know how to tell stories," she says. "A real story has to be in the past."

"As you wish. A robot, then, met a . . ."

"No, no, not that way. A story has to be told like a story. Or else nobody knows it's a story."

She is probably right. I think it over for a moment, unaccustomed to that manner of speech, and I start again:

"Once upon a time, in the long, long ago, in the fair Kingdom of France, a robot who was very intelligent, even though strictly metallic, met at a royal ball a young and lovely lady of the nobility. They danced together. He whispered sweet nothings in her ear. She blushed. He apologized.

"By and by, they danced again. She thought he was a bit rigid, but charming with his stiff manners,

45

which gave him a great deal of distinction. They were married the very next day. They received sumptuous wedding presents and departed on their honeymoon. . . . Is it okay this way?"

"It's no great shakes," says Marie, "but it will do. In any case, you're telling it like a real story."

"Then, I'll go on. The bride, whose name was Blanche, as compensation, because she had raven black hair, the bride, I said, was naïve, and she did not notice right away that her spouse was a product of cybernetics. Yet, she could see that he would always make the same gestures and that he would always say the same things. Well, she thought, here is a man who knows how to follow up on his ideas.

"But one fine morning, having risen earlier than was her custom, she saw him oiling the mechanism of his coxo-femoral articulations, in the bathroom, with the oil can from the sewing machine. Since she was well bred, she made no remark. From that day on, however, doubt invaded her heart.

"Small, unexplained details now came back to her mind: nocturnal creaking sounds, for example, which couldn't really come from the box spring, while her husband embraced her in the secrecy of their alcove; or else the curious ticktock that filled the air around him.

"Blanche had also discovered that his gray eyes, rather inexpressive, would sometimes light up and blink, to the left or to the right, like a car about to change direction. Other signs, as well, mechanical in nature, eventually increased her concern to the utmost.

"Finally, she became certain of even more disturbing peculiarities, and truly diabolical ones: her husband never forgot anything. His stupefying memory, concerning the slightest daily events, as well as the inexplicable rapidity of the mental calculations he effected at the end of each month, when they would check their household accounts together, gave Blanche a treacherous idea. She wanted to know more, and conceived then a Machiavellian plan. . . ."

The children, meanwhile, have both emptied their plates. As for me, I am burning with impatience, anxious as I am to leave this café, and to know at last where we are going next. I rush my conclusion accordingly.

"Unfortunately," I say, "the Seventeenth Crusade broke out right at that moment, and the robot was drafted into the colonial infantry, third armored regiment. He embarked at the port of Marseilles and went to fight the war, in the Near East, against the Palestinians.

"Since all the knights wore articulated stainless steel armor, the physical peculiarities of the robot passed henceforth unnoticed. And he never returned to Sweet France, for he died absurdly, one summer night, without attracting anyone's attention, under the ramparts of Jerusalem. The poisoned arrow of an Infidel had pierced his helmet and caused a short circuit inside his electronic brain."

Marie pouts:

"The ending is idiotic," she says. "You had a few good ideas, but you did not know how to exploit them intelligently. And, above all, you never succeeded, at any time, in giving life to your characters or in making them sympathetic. When the hero dies, at the end, the audience is not moved at all."

"When the hero expired, wast thou not moved?" I joke.

This time, I did win at least a pretty smile of amusement from my too demanding professor of narration. She answers in the same tone of parody:

"I had, nonetheless, a certain pleasure in listening to thee, my dear, when thou recounted the ball whereat they met and courted. When we had consumed our repast, Jean and I deplored it, for that curtailed thy story: We could divine thy sudden haste at that point. . . ." Then, changing her tone: "Later, I want to study to become a heroine in novels. It is a good job, and it allows one to live in the literary style. Don't you thinks that's prettier?"

"I'm still hungry," says her brother at that point. "Now, I want a pizza."

It must be a joke, for they both laugh. But I don't understand why. It must be part of their private folklore. There follows a very long silence which feels to me like a hole in time or like a blank space between two chapters. I conclude that something new will probably happen. I wait.

My young companions seem to wait, too. Marie takes up her knife and her fork, and she plays for a moment at balancing them, one against the other, by placing the ends together; then she arranges them in a cross in the center of the table. She puts such seriousness into these innocuous exercises, such calculated precision, that they acquire in my eyes the value of cabalistic signs.

I, unfortunately, do not know how to interpret these figures. And perhaps they have no real significance. Marie, like all children and poets, enjoys playing with sense and nonsense. Having completed her construction, she smiles to herself. Jean drinks up the rest of his glass. They are both silent. What are they waiting for like this? It is the boy who breaks the silence:

"No, he says, "have no fear. The pizza, that was just to get a rise out of you. Anyway, it's been several months that in this café they sell only *croque-monsieur* and sandwiches. You were wondering what we were waiting for here, right? The time to get going had not come, that's all. Now, we are going to leave."

Just like his sister, this boy expresses himself almost like an adult. He, furthermore, seems more respectful. He hasn't spoken that many words since I saw him for the first time more than an hour ago. But now, I have understood why he remained so obstinately silent.

His voice is, indeed, in the midst of changing; and he fears seeming ridiculous because of the cracks which happen, unexpectedly, in the middle of his sentences. That might also explain, perhaps, why his sister and he were laughing: the word *pizza* must con-

49

tain sounds that are especially fearsome to his vocal chords.

Marie then supplies me, at last, with the next phase of our program: she herself has to go back home (what home?) to do her homework (homework in lying?), while her brother takes me to a secret meeting, where I am to receive precise instructions. But I must, for my part, remain ignorant of the locale of that appointment. I am therefore going to be disguised as a blind man, with totally opaque, black glasses.

The precautions and mysteries, maintained around its activities by this clandestine organization, are becoming more and more extravagant. But I am convinced that it is largely a game and, in any case, I have decided to pursue the experiment to its end. It is easy to guess why.

I pretend therefore to see nothing strange in the quasimiraculous appearance of the objects necessary to my disguise: the aforementioned goggles, as well as a white cane. Jean has quite naturally gone to pick them up in a corner of the café room, where they were waiting, very close to the spot where we were eating.

The two children had evidently chosen that table, inconvenient and poorly lit, because of its immediate proximity to their hiding place. But who put those props there? Jean, or Marie, or else the student in the red jacket?

That girl must have followed me since I left the workshop with the mannequins, where Djinn engaged me in her service. She could have brought the cane and the glasses already. She followed me to that café, which she entered a few seconds after me. She may have immediately placed these objects in this corner, before sitting at a table close to mine.

Yet, I am surprised to have noticed nothing of these comings and goings. When I discovered her presence, the student was already sitting and quietly reading her big anatomy textbook. But I was indulging, at that moment, in amorous reveries, vague and euphoric, which probably numbed my sense of the realities.

Another question perplexes me even further. It was I who decided to have a cup of coffee in this particular café, the phony student did nothing but follow me in. As it happens, I could, as well, have chosen another establishment on the avenue (or even drink no coffee). How, under these conditions, were the children forewarned, by their accomplice, of the spot where they were going to find the cane and the glasses?

On the other hand, Marie was talking to the waiter, upon our arrival, as though she knew him very well. And Jean knew which dishes were available, among those which are listed, more or less misleadingly, on the sign hanging above the bar. Finally, they claimed their mother was going to come soon, to pay the bill for our meal; whereas all they had to do was let me pay that modest sum myself. The waiter voiced no objection. He visibly trusts these children, who behave like regular customers.

51

Everything happens, therefore, as if I had walked, by chance, precisely into the café they use as their canteen and headquarters. That's rather unlikely. However, the other possible explanation seems stranger still: it wasn't "by chance"; I have, on the contrary, been led, unaware, to this bistro by the organization itself, in order to meet the student who awaited me there.

But, in that case, how have I been "led"? In what manner? By means of what mysterious method? The more I think about it all, the less clear things become, and the more I conclude the presence here of an enigma. . . .

If I could first solve the problem of the connection between the children and the medical student . . . Unfortunately, I solve nothing at all.

While I turned these thoughts over in my head, Jean and his sister adjusted the black goggles over my eyes. The rubber rims of the frames fitted perfectly to my forehead, my temples, my cheekbones. I immediately realized that I could see neither to the sides, nor down below, and neither could I distinguish anything through the lenses, which are really opaque.

And now, we are walking on the sidewalk along the avenue, side by side, the kid and I. We are holding each other by the hand. With my free hand, my right one, I point the white cane forward, its sharp point sweeping the space in front of me, searching for possible obstacles. After a few minutes, I am using this accessory with complete ease.

52

I reflect, while allowing myself to be guided like a blind man, upon this curious progressive deterioration of my freedom, since walking, at half past six in the evening, into the hangar with the mannequins, crowded with cast-off merchandise and junked machinery, where "Monsieur Jean" had asked me to report.

There, not only did I agree to obey the orders of a girl my age (or even younger than I), but furthermore, I did so under the insulting threat of a revolver (a hypothetical one at least), which destroyed any impression of voluntary choice. Moreover, I accepted without a word of protest, this total ignorance of my exact mission and of the goals sought by the organization. I wasn't bothered in the least by any of that: I did, on the contrary, feel happy and lighthearted.

Next, a rather ungracious student, in a café, forced me, with her air of a school inspector, or of a teacher, to take a path that did not seem the best to me. This led me to having to care for a supposedly injured boy, who was lying unconscious on the ground, but who in fact was making a fool of me.

When I found out, I did not complain of this unfairness. And I soon saw myself obeying, this time, a girl barely ten years old, a liar and a compulsive one at that. In the last place, I ended up by agreeing to relinquish as well the use of my eyes, after having in succession given up that of my free choice and that of my intelligence.

Things have reached the point where I now behave without understanding anything of what I am doing, or of what is happening to me, without even knowing where I am going, entrusted to the lead of this taciturn child who is perhaps an epileptic. And I seek in no way to infringe upon the orders received, by cheating a little with the black glasses. It is probably enough to push the frames slightly, as though I were scratching my eyebrow, so as to create a space between the rubber rim and my nose. . . .

But I undertake no such thing. I have willingly become an irresponsible agent. I did not fear to let myself be blindfolded. Soon, if it pleases Djinn, I shall myself become some sort of rudimentary robot. I can already picture myself, in a wheelchair, blind, mute, deaf . . . and what else yet?

I smiled to myself at that image.

"Why do you laugh?" asks Jean.

I answer that my present situation seems to me rather comical. The boy takes up, then, as a quote, a phrase I have already heard from the lips of his sister, while we were in the café:

"Love," he says, "it makes one do great things."

At first, I thought he was making fun of me, and I answered, with a certain annoyance, that I couldn't see the relationship. But, upon reflection, this remark of his seems to me above all inexplicable. How would he know of this hoped-for love (quasi-absurd and, in any case, secret) that I have barely acknowledged to myself?

"Oh, but yes," he goes on in that voice of his that

54

wavers constantly between low and sharp, "there is an obvious relationship: love is blind, that's well known. And, in any case, you mustn't laugh: being blind, that's sad."

I am going to ask him if he concludes therefore that love is sad (which seems the evident conclusion, in a perfect syllogism, of his two propositions concerning the status of the blind), when there occurs an event that puts an end to our conversation.

We had stopped, for a few moments, at the edge of a sidewalk (I had felt the stone edge with the iron tip of my cane) and I had thought that we were waiting for the traffic light that gives pedestrians the right to cross. (We do not have a musical signal for the blind, as is the case in many cities in Japan.) But I was mistaken. This place must have been a taxi stand, where Jean waited for the arrival of a free cab.

He helped me, as a matter of fact, to climb into a car, a fairly large one, it seems, judging by the width of the doors that I negotiate gropingly (I have relinquished my cane to my guide). I settle down on what seems to be the rear seat, spacious and comfortable.

While I was sitting down, Jean slammed the door, and he must have walked around the car, in order to climb in himself through the left door: I can hear it open, and someone getting in and sitting next to me. And that someone is the kid, all right, for his voice, with its inimitable cracks, says, in the direction of the driver:

"We are going here, please."

I can make out at the same time the slight rustling of paper. Instead of saying aloud where we wish to go, Jean has most likely handed the driver a piece of paper on which the address has been written (by whom?). Such subterfuge allows them to leave me ignorant of our destination. Since it is a child using it, this method can't surprise the driver.

And suppose it wasn't a taxi?

CHAPTER FIVE

While the car rolled on, I thought again about the absurdity of my situation. But I did not succeed in making the decision to put an end to it. This obstinacy of mine surprised me. I blamed myself for it, all the while complacently enjoying it. The interest that I harbor for Djinn could not be its only cause. There also had to be, quite certainly, curiosity. And what else yet?

I felt pulled along in a chain of episodes and encounters, in which chance probably played no part at all. I was the only one who did not grasp its profound causality. These successive mysteries made me think of a sort of treasure hunt: one progresses from clue to clue, and discovers the solution only at the very end. And the treasure, it was Djinn!

I wondered, as well, about the kind of work the organization expected of me. Were they afraid to tell me openly about it? Was it so disreputable a job? What was the meaning of these endless preliminaries? And why did they leave me so little initiative in the matter?

This total absence of information, I hoped just the same that it was only temporary: perhaps I was first supposed to pass through this initial phase, where I would be put to the test. The treasure hunt thus became, in my romantic mind, like a journey of initiation.

As for my recent transformation into this classic character of a blind man led by a child, it was meant no doubt to arouse people's sympathy, and thereby put their suspicions to rest. But, as for passing unnoticed in the crowd, as I had been sternly instructed to, it seemed to me a very dubious way.

Beyond that, a precise subject of concern kept coming back to preoccupy me: where were we going now? Which streets, which boulevards were we following? Towards which suburbs were we thus driving? Towards what revelation? Or else, toward what new secret? Was the trip to get there going to be long?

This last point above all—the length of the car ride—nagged at me, without a specific reason. Perhaps Jean was authorized to tell me? Taking a chance, I asked him about it. But he answered that he had no idea himself, which seemed even stranger to me (inasmuch, at least, as I believed it).

The driver, who could hear all we were saying, then intervened to reassure me:

"Don't worry. We'll get there soon."

But instead, I perceived, in these two sentences, a vague threat I couldn't explain. In any case, it didn't mean much. I listened to the sounds of the street, around us, but they provided no indication of the sections of town we were driving through. Perhaps, however, the traffic here was less intense.

Next, Jean offered me a mint lozenge. I answered that I would take one. But it was rather out of courtesy. So, he touched my left arm, saying:

"Here, give me your hand."

I offered it to him, my palm extended. He placed in it a piece of half melted candy, sort of sticky, like all children carry in their pockets. I really didn't feel at all like it anymore, but I dared not confess it to the donor: once I had accepted the candy, it became impossible to return it.

So I put it into my mouth, quite against my will. I immediately thought it had a weird taste, flat and bitter at the same time. I felt very much like spitting it out again. I abstained, once more to spare the kid's feelings. For, unable to see him, I could never know

59

whether he was not precisely watching me at that very moment.

I was discovering here a paradoxical consequence of blindness: a blind person can no longer do anything secretly! Those poor people who can't see constantly fear being seen. In order to escape this unpleasant feeling, in a rather illogical reflex, I closed my eyes behind my black glasses.

I slept, I am sure of it; or, at least, I dozed off. But I don't know for how long.

"Wake up," said the kid's voice, "we're getting off here."

And he was shaking me lightly, at the same time. I now suspect that mint lozenge, with its suspicious flavor, was drugged with sleeping medicine; for I am hardly in the habit of falling asleep this way in cars. My friend Jean has drugged me, that is most likely, just as he must have been ordered to. This way, I won't even know the length of the trip we have just taken.

The car has stopped. And my youthful guide has already paid the fare (if, however, it is really a cab, which seems to me to be less and less certain). I no longer sense any presence in the driver's seat. And I have the confused feeling that I am no longer in the same car.

I find it hard to regain my wits. The darkness in which I am still steeped makes waking even more difficult, and also leaves it more uncertain. I have a feeling that my sleep continues, while I dream that I am coming out of it. Furthermore, I no longer have the slightest idea of the time.

"Hurry. We are not early."

My guardian angel is growing anxious and lets me know straightaway, in his funny voice that goes off-key. I extract myself with difficulty from the car, and I stand as well as I can. I feel quite woozy, as though I had been drinking too much.

"Now," I say, "give me back my cane."

The kid places it in my right hand, and then he grabs the left one to pull me vigorously along.

"Don't go so fast. You're going to make me lose my balance."

"We're going to be late, if you drag your feet."

"Where are we going now?"

"Don't ask me. I'm not allowed to tell you. And besides, it doesn't have a name."

The place is, at any rate, quite silent. It seems to me that there is no longer anyone around us. I can hear neither voices nor footsteps. We are walking on gravel. Then the feeling of the ground changes. We step over a threshold and we enter a building.

There, we follow a rather complex course the kid seems to know by heart, for he never hesitates when changing direction. A wooden floor has replaced the stone of the entryway.

Possibly, there is someone else, now, who is walking beside us, or rather ahead of us, to show us the way. Indeed, if I stop for a second, my young guide, who holds me by the hand, stops also, and I seem then to detect, just ahead, a third footstep that continues for a few seconds more. But it is difficult to say for sure.

"Don't stop," says the kid.

And a few feet farther:

"Pay attention, we're coming to some stairs. Take the banister in your right hand. If your cane is in the way, give it to me."

No, instinctively, I prefer not to relinquish it. I can sense a danger of sorts closing in on us. So I grasp, with the same hand, the iron banister and the curved handle of the cane. I stand ready for any eventuality. If something too disquieting happens, I am getting ready to suddenly pull my black goggles off with my left hand (which the kid holds rather loosely in his own), and to brandish, with the right, my iron tipped cane to serve as a defensive weapon.

But no alarming event occurs. After having climbed one floor, up a very steep staircase, we soon arrive at a room where a meeting, it seems, is in progress. Jean has warned me before walking in, adding in a whisper:

"Don't make any noise. We are the last ones. Let's not get ourselves noticed."

He has softly opened the door, and I follow him, still led by the hand, like a small child. There is a crowd in the room: I can tell right away because of the very faint—but numerous—assorted sounds, breathing, suppressed coughing, the rumpling of fabric, slight impacts or furtive sliding sounds, soles imperceptibly scraping the floor, etc.

Yet, all these people remain motionless, I am convinced of it. But they have probably remained standing, and they move a little in place, that can't be helped. Since I haven't been shown a seat, I remain standing, too. Around us, no one says anything.

And suddenly, in this silence quickened by many attentive presences, the long-awaited surprise comes at last. Djinn is here, in the room, her lovely voice rises a few feet from me. And I feel, suddenly, rewarded for all my patience.

"I have gathered you here," she says, "in order to give you some explanations, henceforth necessary. . . ."

I imagine her at a podium, standing as well, and facing her audience. Is there a table in front of her, as in a classroom? And how is Djinn dressed? Is she still wearing her raincoat and her felt hat? Or else, has she taken them off for this meeting? What about her dark glasses, has she kept them on?

For the first time, I am dying to remove mine. But nobody has yet give me permission; and this is not after all the right moment, with all these people nearby who can see me. Not counting Djinn herself . . . I must therefore be satisfied with what is offered me: the delicious voice with its hint of an American accent.

". . . clandestine international organization . . . partitioning the tasks . . . great humanitarian enterprise . . ."

What great humanitarian enterprise? What is she talking about? Suddenly, I become aware of my frivolity: I'm not even listening to what she says! Charmed by her exotic intonations, quite busy imagining the face and the mouth from which they come (is she smiling? Or else is she putting on that phony gang-leader look?), I have forgotten the main thing: to pay attention to the information contained in her words; I am savoring them instead of registering their meaning. And all the time, I claimed to be so anxious to learn more about my future work!

But now, Djinn has stopped speaking. What has she just said, exactly? I try in vain to remember. I have the vague idea that they were only words of greeting, of welcome into the organization, and that the most important part remains yet to come. But why is she silent? And what are the other members of the audience doing in the meantime? Nobody moves around me, nor evidences any surprise.

I don't know if it's emotional, but a bothersome itching is annoying my right eye. Vigorous blinking does not succeed in getting rid of it. I try to find a way to scratch discreetly. My left hand has remained held in the kid's, and he is not letting go, and the right one is encumbered with the cane. Yet, unable to stand it any longer, I attempt with that right hand to rub at least the area around my eye.

Inconvenienced by the curved handle of the cane, I make a clumsy gesture, and the thick frame of the glasses slides upward, to my eyebrows. As a matter of fact, the goggles have barely moved, but the space created between my skin and the rubber rim is still enough to allow me to glimpse what is directly on my right. . . .

It leaves me stupefied. I had hardly guessed anything like this. . . . I slowly move my head, in order to sweep a wider angle through my narrowed field of vision. What I see, on all sides, only confirms my initial stupefaction: I have the feeling that I am in front of my own image, multiplied twenty or thirty-fold.

The entire room is, in fact, full of blind men, phony blind men as well, most likely: young men my own age, dressed in various ways (but, all in all, pretty much like me), with the same heavy black goggles over their eyes, the same white cane in the right hand, a kid just like mine holding them by the left hand.

They are all turned in the same direction, toward the stage. Each pair—a blind man and his guide—is separated from the others by an empty space, always about the same, as if one had taken care to arrange, on carefully marked squares, a series of identical statuettes.

And, suddenly, a stupid feeling of jealousy tightens my heart: It isn't me then that Djinn was speaking to! I did know she was addressing a large assembly. But it is quite something else to see, with my own eyes, that Djinn has already recruited two or three dozen guys, who are little different from me and treated in exactly the same way. I am nothing more, to her, than the least remarkable among them.

But just at that moment, Djinn resumes speaking. Most strangely, she picks up her speech right in the middle of a sentence, without repeating the words that came before so as to preserve the coherence of her remarks. And she says nothing to justify this interruption; her tone is exactly the same as if there had not been any.

". . . will allow you not to awaken suspicions . . ."

Having abandoned all prudence (and all obedience to the orders that I suddenly can't bear any longer), I manage to turn my head sufficiently, by twisting my neck and raising my chin, so as to place the center of the stage in my visual field. . . .

I don't understand right away what's going on. . . . But soon I must surrender to the evidence: there is a lecturer's table all right, but no one behind it! Djinn is not there at all, nor anywhere else in the room.

It is just a loudspeaker that is broadcasting her address, recorded I know not where nor when. The machine is placed on the table, perfectly visible, almost indecent. It had probably stopped, following some technical trouble: a technician is just now checking the wires, which he must have just plugged back in. . . .

All the charm of that fresh and sensuous voice

has disappeared suddenly. No doubt the rest of the recording is of the same excellent quality; the words continue their lilting song from beyond the Atlantic; the tape recorder faithfully reproduces its sonorities, the melody, down to the slightest inflection. . . .

But, now that the illusion of her physical presence has vanished, I have lost all feeling of contact with that music, so sweet to my ears a moment before. My discovery of the ruse has broken the magical spell of the speech, which has then become dull and cold: the magnetic tape now reels it off with the anonymous neutrality of an airport announcement. So much so that, now, I no longer have any trouble at all listening to its words nor discovering meaning in them.

The faceless voice is in the process of explaining to us our roles and our future functions. But she does not divulge them entirely, she gives us only their broad outlines. She elaborates more on the goals to be pursued than on the methods: it is because of a concern for efficiency that she prefers, she says again, to divulge to us, for the moment, only that which is strictly necessary.

I have not followed well, as I said, the beginning of her exposé. But it seems to me however that I have grasped the essentials: what I am now hearing allows me in any case to assume that I did, for I can find in it no major obscurities (except those intentionally worked in there by the speaker).

We have then, she informs us, been enlisted, the

others and I, in an international movement of struggle against machinism. The classified ad that led me (after a brief exchange of letters, with a post-office box) to meet Djinn in the abandoned workshop, had already led me to assume it as much. But I had not fully fathomed the consequences of the slogan being used: "For a life more free and rid of the imperialism of machines."

In fact, the organization's ideology is rather simple, simplistic even or so it seems: "The time has come to free ourselves from machines, for they, and nothing else, oppress us. Men believe that machines work for them. While men, on the contrary, henceforth work for machines. More and more, machines command us, and we obey them.

"Machinism, above all, is responsible for the division of work into tiny fragments devoid of all meaning. The automated tool demands the performance by each worker of a single gesture, he must repeat from morning to night, all his life long. Fragmentation is evident then in manual work. But it is also becoming the rule in any other branch of human activity.

"This, in all cases, the long-term product of our work (manufactured goods, service, or intellectual study) escapes us entirely. The worker never knows either the form of the whole, or its ultimate use, except in a theoretical and purely abstract way. No responsibility accrues to him, no pride can he reap from it. He is nothing but an infinitesimally small link in the immense chain of production, bringing only a modification of detail to a spare part, to an isolated cog, that have no significance in themselves.

"No one, in any domain, any longer produces anything complete. And man's conscience and awareness have been shattered. But mark my word: it is our alienation by the machine that has brought forth capitalism and Soviet bureaucracy, and not the contrary. It is the atomization of the entire universe that has begotten the atomic bomb.

"Yet, at the beginning of this century, the ruling class, the only one to be spared, still kept decision-making power. Henceforth, the machine that thinks—that is to say, the computer—has taken these away as well. We are no longer anything more than slaves, working toward our own destruction, in the service—and for the greater glory—of the Almighty God of the Mechanical."

On the subject of the means for raising the consciousness of the masses, Djinn is more discreet and less explicit. She speaks of "peaceful terrorism" and "dramatic" actions staged by us in the midst of the crowd, in the subway, in city squares, in offices and in factories. . . .

And yet, something disturbs me about these fine words: it is the fate meant for us, we, the agents of the program's execution: our role is in total contradiction to the goals that it proposes. Up to now at least, this program has hardly been applied to us. We, on the contrary, have been manipulated, without any regard for our free will. And now still, it has been admitted that only partial knowledge of the whole is permitted us. They want to raise our consciousness, but they start out by preventing us from seeing. Finally, to top it all off, it's a machine that talks to us, persuading us, directing us. . . .

Once again, I am filled with mistrust. I sense some unknown, obscure danger floating over this trumped-up meeting. This roomful of phony blind men is a trap, in which I have allowed myself to be caught. Through the narrow slit, which I have carefully maintained under the right edge of my cumbersome glasses, I glance at my closest neighbor, a tall blond guy who wears a white leather windbreaker, rather chic, open over a bright blue pullover. . . .

He has also (as I suspected a moment ago), managed to slip by a fraction of an inch the tight-fitting contraption that blinded him, so as to glimpse the surroundings on his left; in such a way that our sidelong glances have crossed, I am certain of it. A slight tightening of his mouth gives me, besides, a sign of connivance. I return it, in the form of the same grimace, which can pass for a smile in his direction.

The kid who accompanies him, and who holds his left hand, has noticed nothing of our carryings-on, it seems to me. Little Jean hasn't either, certainly, for he, he is clearly located outside this limited exchange. Meanwhile, the harangue goes on, calling out to us in no uncertain terms:

"The machine is watching you: fear it no longer!

The machine gives you orders: obey it no longer! The machine demands all your time: surrender it no longer! The machine thinks itself superior to men: prefer it over them no longer!"

At this point, I see that the character in the white zippered jacket, who has like me kept his blind man's cane in his right hand, slips it discreetly behind his back, toward his left, so as to bring its sharp tip closer to me. With that iron tip, he noiselessly draws complicated signs on the ground.

Indeed, this colleague of mine, as rebellious as I, is trying to communicate something to me. But I can't seem to understand what he wants to tell me. He repeats several times for me the same series of short, straight lines and intertwining curves. I persist vainly in my attempts to decipher them; my very limited view of the floor, distorted furthermore by the excessive angle, doesn't help, that's for sure.

"We have discovered," the recorded voice goes on, "a simple solution to save our brothers. Make them aware of it. Put it in their head without telling them, almost without their knowing it. And turn them themselves into new propagandists . . ."

At this point, I sense a sudden agitation behind me. Hurried footsteps, very near, break the silence. I feel a violent shock, at the base of my skull, and a very sharp pain. . . .

CHAPTER SIX

Simon Lecoeur awoke, feeling hung over, as though he had drunk too much, in the midst of piled-up crates and junked machinery. He regained consciousness little by little, with the vague feeling that he was coming out of a long nightmare. Soon, he recognized the scene around him. It was the abandoned workshop where he had met Djinn. And, almost immediately, there returned to his mind the starting point of his mission.

"I must," he thought, "go to the Gare du Nord.

In fact, I must hurry, for it is most important that I be on time for the arrival of the train from Amsterdam. If I do not creditably carry out this first assignment, I very much fear that I won't be trusted later on, and that I won't be allowed to go any further. . . ."

But Simon Lecoeur felt, in some confused way, that all this business of railroad station, a train, a traveler he was supposed not to miss, was out of date, done with: this future already belonged to the past. Something was scrambling space and time. And Simon did not seem able to define in it all his own situation. What had happened to him? And when? And where?

On the one hand, he was finding himself lying on the floor, unable to grasp the reason for it, in the dust and assorted debris that littered the workshop, among the discarded materials and machinery. On the other hand, it was broad daylight. The sun, already high, of a fine spring morning, brightly illumined from outside the dusty panes of the skylight; while, on the contrary, night had been falling when Djinn materialized, in these same forlorn premises, with her raincoat and her fedora. . . .

Simon suddenly remembered a recent scene, seeing it again with extreme precision: a boy of about ten, probably dead, considering his total immobility, his excessive rigidity and his waxen complexion, who was lying on an iron bedstead with a bare mattress, a large crucifix placed on his chest, under the flickering light of the three candles in a brass candelabrum. . . .

Another image followed this one, just as sharp and swift: that same boy, still clad in the fashion of the last century, was leading a blind man, holding his left hand. The invalid tightly held, in his other hand, the curved handle of a white cane, which he used to reconnoiter the ground in front of his steps. Heavy black goggles half hid his face. He wore a fine white leather windbreaker with a zipper, wide open over a bright blue sweater. . . .

A sudden thought crossed Simon Lecoeur's mind. He felt his chest with his hand. His fingers did not find the ebony crucifix (although he himself was lying supine in the exact position of the kid at the wake), but he acknowledged the presence of the lambskin windbreaker and the cashmere pullover. He recalled having chosen them, in fact, for tonight's appointment, although this blue and white outfit, at once elegant and casual, did not seem to him perfectly suited to job hunting. . . .

"But of course," he said to himself, "this cannot be tonight's meeting. Tonight hasn't come yet, and the appointment has already taken place. Therefore, it must have been last night. . . . As for those two scenes in which the same kid figures, the second one had to take place before the first, since, in the first, the child is lying on his deathbed. . . . But where do these images come from?

Simon did not know whether he should grant them the status of recollections, as though they were events of his real life; or else whether they were not, instead, images such as are shaped in dreams and file through our head at the moment of awakening and usually in reverse chronological order.

In any case, there was a gap in his timetable. Indeed, it seemed hard to conceive that Simon might have slept more than twelve hours in that uncomfortable place . . . unless sleeping pills, or harder drugs, were the cause. . . .

A new image, come from he knew not where, arose unexpectedly in his disordered memory: a long straight alleyway, badly paved, feebly lit by old-fashioned streetlights, between ramshackle fencing, blind walls, and half-ruined cottages. . . . And again, the same kid, springing forth from one of the houses, taking five or six running steps, and sprawling headlong into a puddle of reddish water. . . .

Simon Lecoeur stood up painfully. Every joint hurt, he was uncomfortable, his head heavy. "I must have a cup of coffee," he thought, "and take an aspirin." He recalled having seen, on his way down the broad avenue nearby, a number of coffee shops and restaurants. Simon made a few swipes, with the flat of his hands, at the white fabric of his trousers, now rumpled, shapeless and stained with black dust; but he did not manage, evidently, to restore its normal look.

Turning around to leave, he saw that someone else was lying on the floor, a few yards from him, in an identical position. The body was not wholly visible: a large size crate was hiding from view the upper torso and the head. Simon approached cautiously. He was startled to discover the face: it was Djinn's without the least possible doubt.

The girl was lying across the passageway, still wearing her buttoned-up raincoat, her sunglasses, and her slouch felt hat, which had strangely remained in place when she had dropped, mortally wounded in the back by some knife blade or bullet of a gun. She showed no visible wound, but a puddle of blood, already coagulated, had formed under her chest and had spread onto the darkish concrete floor all around her left shoulder.

Minutes ran out slowly before Simon decided to make a move. He was standing there, motionless, uncomprehending, and inspired with no idea of what he should do. At length, he bent down, overcoming his revulsion, and wanting to touch the hand of the cadaver. . . .

Not only was the hand stiffened and cold, but it seemed to him much too hard, too rigid, to pass as one made of flesh and human joints. In order to dissipate his last doubts, and although an inexplicable revulsion still held him back, he forced himself to feel as well the limbs, the chest, the skin of the cheeks and the lips. . . .

The obvious artificiality of the whole thing quite convinced Simon of his mistake, which duplicated, after all, given the interval of a few hours, the one he had made upon his arrival: he was once more in the presence of a papier-mâché mannequin. Yet, the dark red puddle was not plastic: Simon verified, with his fingertips, its slightly damp and viscous quality. One could not swear, nonetheless, that it was real blood.

All this seemed absurd to Simon Lecoeur; yet, he feared, in some obscure way, that there might be a precise meaning to these simulations, although that meaning eluded him. . . . The murdered mannequin was lying at the exact place where Djinn had stood at the time of the brief interview of the previous day; although Simon remembered very well having seen it, at that time, on the ground floor. . . . Unless he was now confusing the two consecutive scenes, the one with Djinn and the one with the mannequin.

He decided to get out as fast as possible, for fear other enigmas might come to complicate the problem further. As it was, he had already enough of them for several hours of reflection. But, at any rate, the more he thought it over, the less he could find the guiding thread.

He went downstairs. On the ground floor, the facsimile of Djinn was still in its place, casually leaning against the same crates, both hands in the pockets of her trench coat, an imperceptible smile frozen on her waxen lips. The figure upstairs was, therefore, a second mannequin, in all respects identical. The thin mocking smile, on her lips, no longer at all resembled Jane Frank's. Simon had only the unpleasant feeling that someone was making fun of him. He shrugged, and walked to the half-glass door opening onto the courtyard.

. . . Even before he had passed the door, the phony mannequin straightened up a little, and her smile widened. The right hand came out of the trench-coat pocket, moved up to her face, and slowly removed the dark glasses. . . . The seductive pale green eyes reappeared. . . .

It was Simon himself, who, while on his way, imagined this ultimate mystification. But he didn't bother to turn around, to destroy completely its feeble likelihood, so certain did he remain that he had, this time seen only a waxwork American girl. He crossed the yard, passed through the outside gate; then, at the very end of the alley, he turned, as expected, onto the wide avenue teeming with passersby. Simon felt intensely relieved, as though he were at last returning to the real world, after an interminable absence.

It might have been close to noon, to judge from the position of the sun. Since Simon had not rewound his watch in time, the previous night, it had of course stopped; he had just noticed it. In full possession of himself now, he walked with a brisk step. But he could see no café or bistro, although, in his memory, they were plentiful all along the avenue; cafés, probably, started in fact a little farther on. He walked into the first one he saw.

Simon immediately recognized the place: this was where he had already drunk a black coffee, upon leaving, for the first time, the abandonned workshop. But many patrons had taken up places there today, and Simon had trouble finding a free table. Eventually, he spotted one, in a dark corner, and sat there, facing the room.

The taciturn waiter of the day before, in his white jacket and black trousers, was not on duty today, unless he had gone to the kitchen for some hot dish. A middle-aged woman, wearing a gray smock, was replacing him. She came over to the new arrival to take his order. Simon told her he wanted only a cup of black coffee, very strong, with a glass of tap water.

When she returned, carrying on a tray a small white cup, a carafe and a large glass, he asked her, looking as indifferent as he could, whether the waiter wasn't there today. She didn't answer right away, as though she was thinking the question over; then she said, with something like concern in her voice:

"Which waiter are you talking about?"

"The man in the white jacket, who works here, usually."

"I am always the one who works here," she said. "There is no one else, even during busy hours."

"But yesterday, however, I saw . . ."

"Yesterday, you could not see anything: that was the day we close."

And she walked away, pressured by her work. Her tone of voice was not really unpleasant, but full of weariness, sadness even. Simon observed his surroundings. Was he confusing this establishment with another one similarly arranged?

Putting aside the presence of numerous patrons, workmen and office workers of both sexes, the resemblance was, in any case, disconcerting. The same glazed partition separated the room from the sidewalk, the tables were the same, and lined up in identical fashion. The bottles, behind the bar, were lined up in the same way, and the same signs were posted above the upper row of bottles. One of them offered the same fast foods: sandwiches, *croque-monsieur*, pizza.

"Although they no longer serve pizza here, and haven't for some time," thought Simon Lecoeur. Next, he wondered that such a certainty had come to him, with such sudden conviction. He drank his coffee in a single gulp. Since the posted signs listed the price of pizzas, he could no doubt order some. Why had Simon suddenly believed differently? He evidently possessed no special information that might allow such a thought.

But, while he was examining the other signs posted behind the bar, his attention was drawn to a fairly small photo portrait, framed in black, which had also been hung there, off to the side a little, next to the ordinance forbidding the sale of alcoholic beverages to minors. Seized with a curiosity that he himself couldn't explain every well, Simon Lecoeur stood up, feigning a trip to the men's room, and took a few steps out of his way, in order to pass in front of the photo. There, he stopped, as though by chance, to examine it more closely.

It showed a man about thirty, with strange pale eyes, in the uniform of a naval officer, or more exactly of a noncommissioned officer. The face reminded Simon of something. . . . Suddenly he understood why: it was the waiter who had served him the day before.

80

A sprig of boxwood, slipped under the black wood frame, protruded substantially on the right side. Withered by the years, the dusty stems had lost half their leaves. Under the photograph, in the yellowed margin, someone obviously lefthanded had penned this dedication: "For Marie and Jean, their loving Papa."

"Is it the uniform you find puzzling?" said the waitress.

Simon had not heard her coming. The woman in the gray smock was wiping glasses, behind the counter. She went on:

"That's my father you're looking at. He was a Russian."

Simon, who hadn't noticed it, acknowledged that the uniform, indeed, did not belong to the French navy. But, since the man wasn't wearing his cap, the difference wasn't obvious. In order to say something, he asked, rather stupidly, whether the sailor had died at sea:

"Lost at sea," the lady corrected him.

"And your name is Marie?"

"Of course!" she said with a shrug.

He walked down to the basement level, where the ill-smelling toilets were located. The walls, painted a cream color, were being used by the regulars to inscribe their political opinions, their business appointments and their sexual fantasies. Simon thought that, perhaps, one of these messages was meant for him; for instance, that phone number, insistently repeated, written in red crayon, in every direction: 765-43-21. The figures were, in any case, easy to remember.

Walking back to his seat, his eyes stopped on the recessed angle formed by the imitation wood paneling, just behind the chair he occupied. A white cane, like those used by the blind, was leaning in the corner. That wall, very poorly lit, had not captured his attention when he first arrived. The cane must have been there already. Simon Lecoeur sat down again. As the sad waitress passed by, he beckoned to her:

"I'll have a pizza, please."

"We haven't been serving them for months," answered the gray woman. "The health authorities have forbidden us to sell them."

Simon drained his glass of water and paid for the coffee. He was heading for the door, when he remembered something. "Well," he said to himself, "here I go, forgetting my cane." No other table was close enough to the thing, so that it could not belong to another patron. Simon retraced his steps rapidly, picked up the white cane without hesitation and crossed the crowded room, looking serene, holding it under his left arm. He left, without arousing any suspicion.

In front of the café door, a street vendor was displaying on the sidewalk fake tortoiseshell combs and other assorted cheap merchandise. Although they seemed greatly overpriced to him, Simon Lecoeur bought sunglasses, with very large and very dark lenses. He liked the frames, because of their close fit. The bright spring sun hurt his eyes and he didn't want its slanting rays to penetrate through wide side openings. He immediately put on the glasses; they fit him perfectly.

Without knowing why—simply as a game, perhaps—Simon closed his eyes, sheltered behind the dark lenses, and started to walk, feeling the pavement in front of his feet, with the iron tip of his cane. This gave him a sort of restful feeling.

As long as he remembered the disposition of his surroundings, he was able to progress without too much difficulty, although he was forced to slow down more and more. After about twenty steps, he no longer had any idea of the obstacles around him. He felt completely lost and stopped, but did not open his eyes. His status as a blind man protected him from being jostled.

"Sir, would you like me to help you cross?"

It was a young boy who addressed him thusly. Simon could easily guess his approximate age, because his voice was obviously just beginning to change. The sound originated from a clearly definable level, indicating further the height of the child, with a precision that surprised the phony invalid.

"Yes, thank you," answered Simon, "I would like that."

The boy grabbed his left hand, gently and firmly.

"Wait awhile," he said, "the light is green and cars go fast, on the avenue."

Simon concluded that he must have stopped just at the edge of the sidewalk. He had therefore strayed considerably, in a few yards, from his original direction. Yet, the experiment still attracted him, fascinated him, even; he wanted to carry it out until some insurmountable difficulty put an end to it.

He easily located, with the iron tip, the edge of the stone margin and the difference in level, that he would have to negotiate in order to reach the surface of the street. His own idiotic obstinacy surprised him: "I must have one hell of an Oedipus complex," he thought smiling, while the kid pulled him forward, cars having finally given way to pedestrians. But soon his smile vanished, replaced by this inward thought:

"I mustn't laugh: it is sad to be blind. . . ."

The hazy image of a little girl in a gathered white dress, cinched at the waist with a wide ribbon, after wavering momentarily in an indefinable recollection, finally settles behind the screen of, his closed eyelids. . . .

She stands motionless in the frame of a doorway. It is so dark around her that practically nothing is visible. In the dim light, only the white gauze dress, the blond hair, the pale features emerge. The child carries, in front of her, in both hands, a large three-branched candelabrum, polished and shiny: but its three candles are out.

I wonder, once more, where these images might

come from. This candelabrum has already appeared in my memory. It has been placed on a chair, lit that time, at the head of a young boy lying on his death-bed. . . .

But we have now reached the other side of the street, and I fear that my guide might abandon me. Since I am not yet comfortable in my part as a blind man, I wish that we might continue to walk together, for a few extra minutes. In order to gain time, I question him.

"What's your name?"

"My name is Jean, sir."

"You live around here?"

"No, sir, I live in the fourteenth district."

We are, however, at the other end of Paris. Although there might be a number of reasons to explain the presence here of that child, I am surprised that he wanders around, this way, so far from his home. About to question him on this subject, I suddenly fear that he might find my indiscretion strange, that it might alarm him, and that it could even cause him to flee. . . .

"Rue Vercingétorix," specifies the kid, in that voice of his that breaks from sharp to low, and in the middle of a word as well.

The name of the leader of the Gauls surprises me: I think there is, to be sure, a rue Vercingétorix that opens onto this avenue, and I don't think there is another one elsewhere, not in Paris in any case. It is impossible that the same name would be used for two different streets in the same city, unless there are also two Vercingétorixes in French history. I convey my doubts to my companion.

"No," he answers, without an hesitation, "there is only one Vercingétorix and only one street by that name in Paris. It is in the fourteenth arrondissement."

I must then be confusing it with another street name? . . . It happens rather often this way, that we believe in things that are quite false: it is enough that some fragment of a memory, come from elsewhere, enters into some coherent pattern open to it, or else that we unconsciously fuse two disparate halves, or still that we reverse the order of the elements in some causal system, to fashion in our minds chimerical objects, having for us all the appearances of reality. . . .

But I put off until later the solution to my problem of topography, for fear the kid might eventually tire of my questions. He has let go of my hand, and I doubt that he wants to go on serving as my guide for much longer. His parents are perhaps expecting him for the midday meal.

As he hasn't said anything else for a fairly long time (long enough for me to be aware of it), I even fear for a moment that he has already gone, and that I may, henceforth, have to go on alone, without his providential support. I must look rather forlorn, for I hear his voice, reassuring to me in spite of its strange sonorities.

"It doesn't seem that you're accustomed to walking alone," he says. "Do you want us to stay together a little longer? Where are you going?"

I am at a loss to answer. But I must keep my improvised guide from noticing my embarrassment. In order not to let him find out that I do not myself know where I am going, I answer with assurance, without thinking:

"To the Gare du Nord."

"In that case, we shouldn't have crossed over. That's on the other side of the avenue."

He is right, of course. I give him, again quickly, the only explanation that comes to mind:

"I thought this sidewalk would be less crowded."

"As a matter of fact, it *is* less crowded," says the kid. "But in any case, you were supposed to make a right turn immediately. You're taking the train?"

"No, I am going to meet a friend."

"Where is he coming from?"

"He is coming from Amsterdam."

"At what time?"

I have once again ventured upon dangerous ground. Let's hope there is really such a train in the early afternoon. Fortunately, it is quite unlikely that this child would know the train schedules.

"I don't remember the exact time," I say. "But I am sure that I am quite early."

"The express from Amsterdam pulls into the station at 12:34," says the kid. "We can be there on time if we take the shortcut. Come on. Let's hurry."

CHAPTER SEVEN

"We'll take the alley," says the kid. "It will be faster. But you'll have to be careful where you put your feet: the paving stones are quite uneven. On the other hand, there won't be any more cars or pedestrians."

"Good," I say, "I'll be careful."

"I'll guide you as well as I can between the holes and the bumps. When we come to some particular obstacle, I'll squeeze your hand harder. . . . Well, here we are: we have to turn right."

I'd better open my eyes, of course. It would be safer, and at any rate, more convenient. But I have decided to walk like a blind man for as long as possible. This has to be what is known as a losing bet. It looks, after all, as though I'd be behaving like a scatterbrain or a child, a behavior that is hardly customary for me. . . .

At the same time, this darkness to which I am condemning myself, and which I doubtlessly enjoy, seems to me to fit perfectly the mental uncertainty in which I have been struggling since waking up. My self-imposed blindness would be some sort of metaphor for it, or its objective correlative, or a redundancy. . . .

The kid pulls me vigorously by the left arm. He advances with long steps, light and sure, and I can barely keep pace with their rhythm. I should let go, take more chances, but I don't dare: I feel the ground in front of me with the tip of my cane, as though I feared to find myself suddenly in front of some chasm, which would be, after all, quite unlikely. . . .

"If you don't walk any faster," says the kid, "you won't get there on time for the train, you'll miss your friend, and then we'll have to look for him all over the station."

The time I get there hardly matters to me, and for good reason. Yet, I follow my guide with confidence and earnestness. I have the funny feeling that he is leading me towards something important, of which I know nothing, and which might well have nothing to do with the Gare du Nord and the Amsterdam train.

Propelled, most likely, by this obscure idea, I venture more and more boldly on this surprise-laden ground to which my feet are getting accustomed little by little. Soon, I feel quite comfortable here. I almost feel as if I were swimming in a new element. . . .

I didn't think that my legs would function so easily and by themselves, without control, so to speak. They would like to go even faster still, pulled along by a force in which the kid has no part. I would run, now, if he asked me to. . . .

But it is he who suddenly stumbles. I don't even have time to hold him back, his hand slips out of mine, and I can hear him falling heavily, just in front of me. I could almost, carried along by my impetus, fall too on top of him, and we would roll together in the dark, one on top of the other, like characters out of Samuel Beckett. I burst out laughing at that image, while struggling to regain my balance.

As for my guide, he does not laugh at his misadventure. He doesn't speak a word. I don't hear him move. Could he be injured through some unlikely bad luck? Could his fall have caused some trauma to his skull, his head having hit a raised cobblestone?

I call him by his first name, and I ask him if he's been hurt: but he answers nothing. A great silence has suddenly descended, and it goes on, which is beginning to concern me seriously. I feel the stone with the iron tip of my cane, taking infinite precautions. . . .

The body of the kid lies across our path. He

seems motionless. I kneel down and I bend over him. I let go of my cane in order to feel his clothes with both hands. I get no reaction, but, under my fingers, I feel a sticky liquid, the nature of which I cannot determine.

This time, I am seized by fear for good. I open my eyes. I remove my dark glasses. . . . I remain dazed, at first, by the bright light to which I am no longer accustomed. Then, the surroundings come into focus, become clearer, take on a consistency, as would a Polaroid photograph, where the picture would appear little by little on the glazed white paper. . . . But it is like the setting in a dream, repetitive and full of anguish, with convolutions from which I could not manage to free myself. . . .

The long, deserted street, stretching in front of me, reminds me indeed of something, the origin of which however I could not determine: I only have the feeling of a place where I would already have come, recently, once at least, several times perhaps. . . .

It is a straight alley, fairly narrow, empty, solitary, you can't see the end of it. It looks like it has been abandoned by everyone, quarantined, forgotten by time. Each side is lined with low structures, uncertain, more or less dilapidated: crumbling houses with yawning apertures, ruined workshops, blind walls and ramshackle fences. . . .

On the crude old-fashioned pavement—which has probably not been repaired for a hundred years—

a kid about twelve, clad in a gray smock, billowing and cinched at the waist, such as little boys used to wear last century, lies prone, stretched to his full length, seemingly deprived of consciousness. . . .

All of this then would have taken place already, previously, once at least. This situation, however exceptional, that I confront here, would only be the reproduction of a previous adventure, exactly identical, one whose events I myself would have lived, and in which I play the same part. . . . But when? And where?

Progressively, the memory dims. . . . The more I attempt to close in on it, the more it escapes me. . . . A last glimmer, still. . . . Then nothing more. It will all have been but a brief illusion. I am well acquainted, anyway, with these sharp and fleeting impressions, which I, as well as many others, experience frequently, and which are sometimes called: memory of the future.

It might instead be, in fact, an instantaneous memory: we believe that what is happening to us has already happened before, as though the present time were splitting in two, breaking in its own midst into two parts: an immediate reality, plus a ghost of that reality. . . . But the ghost soon wavers. . . . One would like to grasp it. . . . It passes again and again behind our eyes, diaphanous butterfly or dancing will-o'-the-wisp that toys with us. . . . Ten seconds later, it has all fled forever.

As to the fate of the injured boy, there is, in any

case, one reassuring fact: the viscous liquid that stained my fingers, when I felt the ground close to the gray linen smock, is not blood, although its color could make you think of it, as well as the way it feels.

It is nothing but an ordinary puddle of reddish mud, colored by rusty dust, that has probably remained in the hollow of the pavement since the last rain. The child, luckily for his clothes, which are threadbare, but very clean, has fallen just on the edge. He was trying perhaps to guide me away from that obstacle towards which I was rushing, when he himself lost his balance. I hope the consequence of his fall will not be too serious.

But I ought to do something about it, it is an emergency. Even if nothing is broken, the fact that he has fainted could make me fear some serious injury. And yet, I do not see, as I turn over the frail body with maternal care, any injury to either the forehead or the jaw.

The whole face is intact. The eyes are closed. It looks as though the kid is asleep. His pulse and his breathing seem normal, though very weak. In any case, I have to take action: nobody will come to my help in this deserted place.

If the surrounding houses were lived in, I'd go there to seek assistance. I'd carry the child there, kind women would offer him a bed, and we would call the paramedics, or some neighborhood physician who would be willing to come over.

But are there any tenants in these crumbling

buildings open to the weather? That would surprise me greatly. There ought to be living there, at this point, no one except some vagabonds who would laugh at me were I to ask them for a bed or a telephone. Perhaps even, were I to disturb them in the midst of some suspicious pursuit, they would manage an even worse reception for me.

Just then, I spot, directly on my right, a small two-story building, where the windows have remained in place in their frames and still retain all their panes. The door is ajar. . . . It is there, then, that I shall attempt my first visit. As soon as I have placed the injured boy under some shelter, I will already feel better.

But it seems to me, inexplicably, that I already know the rest: pushing the half open door with my foot, I shall penetrate into that unknown house, with the unconscious child that I shall be holding carefully in my arms. Inside, all will be obscure and deserted. I shall perceive, however, a dim bluish light, which will be coming from the second floor. I shall slowly climb a wooden staircase, steep and narrow, with steps that will creak in the silence. . . .

I know it. I remember it. . . . I remember that entire house, with hallucinating precision, and all those events that would therefore already have taken place, through whose succession I would already have lived, and in which I would have taken an active part. . . . But when was that?

At the very top of the stairs, there was a half-open door. A young woman, tall and slender, with pale blond hair, was standing in the doorway, as though she had been waiting for someone's arrival. She was wearing a white dress, of some light fabric, gauzy, translucent, whose folds, floating at the whim of an unlikely breeze, caught the reflections of that blue light that fell I knew not from where.

An undefinable smile, very gentle, youthful and faraway, played upon her pale lips. Her large green eyes, widened still in the semidarkness, shone with a strange brilliance "like those of a girl who would have come from another world," thought Simon Lecoeur, as soon as he saw her.

And he remained there, motionless on the threshold of the room, holding in his arms ("like an armful of roses offered in tribute," he thought) the unconscious little boy. Struck with enchantment himself, he gazed upon the otherworldly apparition, fearful at each instant that she might disappear in a wisp of smoke, especially when a stronger gust of air (to which yet no other object in the room seemed exposed), blew her veils around her like "ash-colored flames."

After a time, probably very lengthy (but impossible to measure with any certainty), during which Simon did not manage to compose, in his mind, any phrase that might have been appropriate to this extraordinary situation, he finally, for lack of anything better, spoke these ridiculously simple words:

"A child has been hurt."

"Yes, I know," said the young woman, but after such a delay that Simon's words seemed to have traveled, before reaching her, immense distances. Then, after another silence, she added: "Hello. My name is Djinn."

Her voice was soft and faraway, alluring yet elusive, like her eyes.

"You are an elf?" asked Simon.

"A spirit, an elf, a girl, as you like."

"My name is Simon Lecoeur," said Simon.

"Yes, I know," said the strange girl.

She had a slight foreign accent, British perhaps, unless these were the melodious tones of sirens and fairies. Her smile had become imperceptibly more pronounced with these words: it seemed she was speaking from elsewhere, from very far away in time, that she was standing in a sort of future world, in the midst of which everything would already have been accomplished.

She opened the door wide, so that Simon could walk in without difficulty. And she gestured to him gracefully with a movement of her bare arm (which had just emerged out of a very ample and flaring sleeve) toward an old-fashioned brass bed. Its head, resting against the back wall under an ebony crucifix, was framed by two gilt bronze candelabra that sparkled, bearing numerous tapers. Djinn started to light these, one after the other.

"It looks like a deathbed," said Simon.

"Won't all beds be deathbeds, sooner or later?"

answered the young woman in a barely audible whisper. Her voice took on a little more substance to declare, with sudden maternal care: "As soon as you have laid him upon these white sheets, Jean will fall into a dreamless sleep."

"So you even know that his name is Jean?"

"What else would he be called? What strange name would you want him to bear? All little boys are called Jean. All little girls are called Marie. You would know that, if you were from here."

Simon wondered what she meant by the words *from here*. Did she mean this strange house? Or this whole abandoned street? Simon very gently laid the still-inanimate child on the funeral bed. Djinn folded his hands across his chest, as is done for those whose soul is departing.

The child let her without offering the slightest resistance, nor showing any other reaction. His eyes had remained wide open, but his pupils were fixed. The flame of the candles lit them with dancing lights, which imparted to them a feverish, supernatural, disconcerting life.

Djinn, now, stood motionless again, next to the bed she surveyed serenely. To see her there, in her filmy white dress, almost immaterial, she looked like an archangel watching over the repose of a restless heart.

Simon had to shake himself back to reality, in the oppressive silence that had fallen upon the room, to ask the young woman some new questions:

97

"Can you tell me, then, what ails him?"

"He is afflicted," she answered, "with acute dysfunction of the memory, which provokes partial losses of consciousness, and which might end up killing him completely. He should rest, or else his overwrought brain will tire too soon, and his nervous cells will die of exhaustion, before his body reaches adulthood."

"What kind of dysfunction, exactly?"

"He remembers, with extraordinary precision, events that have not yet taken place: what will happen to him tomorrow, or even what he will do next year. And you are, here, nothing but a character out of his afflicted memory. When he wakes up, you will immediately disappear from this room, where, as a matter of fact, you have not yet set foot. . . ."

"So, I will come here at a later date?"

"Yes. Beyond any doubt."

"When?"

"I don't know the exact date. You will walk into this house, for the first time, about the middle of next week. . . ."

"And what about you, Djinn? What would become of you if he woke up?"

"I, too, will disappear from here upon his awakening. We would both disappear at the same time."

"But where would we go? Would we stay together?"

"Oh, no. That would be contrary to the rules of chronology. Try to understand: you will go where you ought to be at that time, in your present reality. . . ."

"What do you mean by *present?*"

"It is your future self that is here by error. Your present day self is several miles away from here, I think, where you are attending some ecological meeting, that opposes electronic machinism, or something of the sort."

"What about you?"

"I, unfortunately, am already dead, and have been for almost three years, so I will not go anywhere. It is only Jean's malfunctioning brain that has brought us together in this house, by chance: I belong to his past, while you, Simon, you belong to his future existence. You understand, now?"

But Simon could not manage to grasp—except as a total abstraction—what all this could mean in the here and now. In order to test whether he was—yes or no—nothing but someone else's dream, it occurred to him to pinch his ear hard. He felt a normal pain, quite real. But what did that prove?

He had to struggle against the vertigo to which these confusions of time and space subjected his reason. This diaphanous and dreamlike woman was perhaps quite insane. . . . He raised his eyes toward her. Djinn was watching him with a smile.

"You pinch your ear," she said, "in order to know whether you are not in the midst of a dream. But you are not dreaming: you are being dreamed, that is quite different. As for me, although I am dead, I can still feel pain and pleasure in my body: these are my past joys and sufferings, recalled by that overly receptive child, and imbued by him with new life, barely dulled by time."

Simon was the prey of contradictory emotions. On the one hand, this strange girl fascinated him, and, without admitting it to himself, he feared to see her disappear; even if she came from the realm of shadows, he wanted to stay close to her. But at the same time, he was angry to hear all that nonsense: he had the feeling that he was being told, to mock him, tales without rhyme or reason.

He tried to reason calmly. This scene (which he was, at that very moment, living) could have belonged to his future existence—or to that of the child—only if the characters present in the room were, indeed, to be gathered there a little later—the following week, for instance. However, that became an impossibility, under normal conditions, if the girl had died three years before.

Owing to the same anachronisms, the scene now taking place here could not have happened in Djinn's past existence, since he had never met her before, while she was alive. . . .

A doubt, suddenly, shook that overly reassuring conviction. . . . In a flash, a recollection crossed Simon's mind, of a past meeting with a blond girl, with pale green eyes and a slight American accent. . . . Soon this impression vanished, suddenly, just as it had come. But it left the young man perturbed.

Had he confused her, for a fleeting moment, with some image of the actress Jane Frank that would have strongly impressed him, in a movie? That explanation was not convincing. A fear seized him, more strongly than ever, that the child would regain consciousness, and that Djinn would vanish before his eyes, forever.

At that moment, Simon became aware of a significant peculiarity in the decor, to which, very strangely, he had not yet paid any attention: the curtains of the room were drawn. Made of some heavy, dark-red fabric, probably quite old (worn threadbare along the folds), they completely masked the window-panes that must have opened onto the street. Why were they kept drawn that way, in broad daylight?

But Simon reflected then on that idea of broad "daylight." What time could it be? Stirred by a sudden anxiety, he ran to the windows, which emitted no light at all, neither through the fabric or along the sides. He hastily raised a fold of the curtain.

Outside, it was pitch black. For how long had it been? The alley was steeped in total darkness, under a starless and moonless sky. Not the slightest light—electric or otherwise—in the windows of the houses, themselves almost invisible. A single old-fashioned streetlight, fairly distant, way off to the right, gave off a faint bluish light in a radius barely a few feet wide.

Simon let the curtain fall back. Would night have fallen that fast? Or else was time flowing "here" according to other laws? Simon looked at his wristwatch. He wasn't even surprised to see that it had stopped. The hands showed exactly twelve o'clock. That was noon as well as midnight.

On the wall, between the two windows, hung a photographic portrait under glass, framed in black wood, with a sprig of boxwood protruding from the back. Simon looked at it more closely. But the light that came from the candelabra was not enough for him to make out the features of the person, a man in some military uniform, it seemed.

A sudden desire to see the face better seized Simon, for whom the image was suddenly taking on an inexplicable significance. He returned quickly to the bed, grabbed one of the candlesticks, and returned to the portrait, which he lighted as best he could with the flickering light of the candles. . . .

He could almost have bet on it: it was his own photograph. No mistake was possible. The face was perfectly recognizable, although older perhaps by two or three years, or barely more than that, which brought to it an expression of seriousness and maturity.

This left Simon petrified. Holding at arm's length the heavy bronze candelabrum, he could not take his eyes off his double, who smiled imperceptibly at him, a smile both fraternal and mocking.

He wore, in that unknown photo, the uniform of the navy and the braid of a chief petty officer. But the costume was not exactly like that worn in the French forces, not at that time, in any case. Simon, furthermore, had never been either a sailor or a soldier. The print was of a sepia tint a little washed out. The paper seemed yellowed by time, marked by small gray and brownish stains.

In the lower margin, two short, handwritten lines slanted across the blank space. Simon immediately recognized his own handwriting, slanted backwards like that of left-handed people. He read in a low voice: "For Marie and Jean, their loving Papa."

Simon Lecoeur turned around. Without his hearing her, Djinn had moved closer to him; and she was gazing upon him with an almost tender, playful pout:

"You see," she said, "that's a photo of you taken a few years from now."

"Then it also belongs to Jean's abnormal memory, and to the future?"

"Of course, as does everything else here."

"Except you?"

"Yes, that's right. Because Jean mixes up times and tenses. That's what confuses things and makes them hard to understand."

"You were saying just now that I would come here a few days hence. Why? What will I come here for?"

"You will bring back an injured little boy in your arms, obviously, a little boy who must, besides, be your son."

"Jean is my son?"

"He 'will be' your son, as proved by the dedication on this photograph. And you will also have a little daughter, who will be called Marie."

"Can't you see that's impossible! I cannot, next

103

week, have an eight-year-old child who is not born today, and whom you would have known, yourself, more than two years ago!"

"You really reason like a Frenchman, positivist and Cartesian. . . . In any case, I said that you would come here in a few days, 'for the first time,' but you will come back many times after that. You will probably even live in this house with your wife and your children. Why, otherwise, would your photo hang on this wall?"

"You are not French?"

"I was not French. I was American."

"What was your occupation?"

"I was a movie actress."

"And what killed you?"

"A machine accident. caused by a crazed computer. That is the reason why I militate now, against mechanization and data processing."

"But what do you mean, 'now'? I thought you were dead!"

"So what? You too, are dead! Didn't you notice the portrait in black wood, and the holy boxwood that watches over your soul?"

"And what did I die from? What would I die from? I mean, what will I die from?" shouted Simon with growing exasperation.

"Lost at sea," replied Djinn calmly.

This was too much. Simon made a last, desperate effort to extricate himself from a situation which could be nothing else but a nightmare. He thought he

104

should first relax his overwrought nerves: he had to scream, he had to hit his head against the walls, break something. . . .

In a rage, he dropped the flickering candelabrum to the floor, and he walked with deliberate step toward that overly desirable woman who was mocking him. He grabbed her. Far from resisting him, she wound her arms around him like a blond octopus, with a sensuousness Simon had hardly expected.

Her flesh was too warm and too sweet to belong to a ghost. . . . She was pulling him toward the bed, from which the little boy had fled, wakened no doubt by the commotion. Upon the floor, the spilled candles continued to burn, threatening to set fire to the curtains. . . .

This is the last clear view of the room that Simon had, before he surrendered to ecstasy.

CHAPTER EIGHT

When I arrived in France, last year, I met, by chance, a guy my age named Simon Lecoeur, who was known as Boris, I never knew why.

I liked him right away. He was rather good-looking, tall for a Frenchman, and above all he had a wild imagination that made him, at every moment, turn daily life and its simplest events into strange, romantic adventures, like those found in science fiction stories.

But I also thought, almost from the start, that I'd no doubt need a lot of patience, at times, if I were willingly to accept his extravagant fabrications; I should even write: his follies. "I'll have to like him enormously," I told myself that first day; "otherwise, very soon, we won't be able to stand each other."

We met in a way that was both weird and ordinary, because of an ad read in a daily newspaper. We were both looking for work: some little part-time job that would allow us to buy, without too much effort, if not the necessities, at least little luxuries. He said he was a student, as am I.

A short ad, then, written in telegraphic style, with somewhat unclear abbreviations, was seeking a y.m. or a y.w. to take care of two children, a boy and a girl. It was probably a matter of looking after them at night, picking them up at school, taking them to the zoo, and other things of that sort. We both showed up at the interview. But nobody else came.

The person placing the ad must, in the meantime, have given up the plan, or else, found through another means, what he needed. The fact is that, Simon and I, finding ourselves face to face, each of us believed, at first, that the other was his eventual employer.

When we discovered that this wasn't the case, and that the person placing the ad had actually stood us up, I was personally rather disappointed. But he, without losing his cool poise for an instant, took pleasure in prolonging his misconception, even starting to speak to me as though I was henceforth to become his boss.

"It wouldn't bother you," I asked him then, "to work for a girl?" He answered that, on the contrary, he liked that very much.

He said "liked," and not "would like," which meant that he was going to play the game. So, I pretended, in turn, to be myself what he was making me out to be, because it seemed amusing to me, especially because I found him droll and charming.

I even added that these children, that he would watch for me, from now on, were a handful: they belonged to a terrorist organization that blew up nuclear power plants . . . It's a stupid idea that, I don't know why, had suddenly occurred to me.

Next, we walked to a café, on the boulevard nearby, where he bought me coffee and a *croque-monsieur*. I wanted to order a pizza, but he launched right away into new tales about that bistro, in which poisoned foods would supposedly have been served to enemy spies in order to get rid of them.

As the waiter wasn't very talkative, morose, with a rather sinister look, Simon claimed that he was a Soviet agent, for whom the two kids were in fact working.

We were both in a very happy mood. We whispered in each other's ear, so the waiter couldn't hear us, like conspirators or lovers. We were amused by everything. Everything seemed to be happening in a singular atmosphere, privileged, almost supernatural.

The coffee was terrible. But my companion explained, quite seriously, that if I kept drinking my coffee too strong, it would cause me to become blind, on account of the pale green color of my eyes. He took advantage of that, of course, to pay me a few conventional compliments on my "mysterious look" and even on "the unearthly brilliance" of my eyes!

I had to go to the Gare du Nord, to meet my friend Caroline, who was due to arrive on the train from Amsterdam. That wasn't very far from the place where we were. Simon, who of course wished to accompany me, proposed that we walk there. Rather I should write: "Simon decided we would walk" for his incessant fantasizing, paradoxically, was joined by a rather strong authoritarianism.

So we set out, happily. Simon did his best to invent all kinds of stories, more or less fantastic, concerning the places we were walking through and the people we came across. But he made us take a strange, complicated path, of which he wasn't sure enough: alleyways more and more deserted, which were, he said, supposed to constitute a shortcut.

We ended up completely lost eventually. I was afraid of being late, and I was finding Simon a great deal less amusing. I was very glad, finally, to be able to jump into a cruising taxicab, whose unexpected presence in that deserted place seemed a godsend to me.

Before leaving my deplorable guide, who was refusing—for extravagant reasons—to climb into that car with me, I nevertheless made a date with him for the next day, under an absurd pretext (intentionally absurd): to resume the visit of that desolate quarter—devoid of any tourist appeal—at exactly the place where we were parting company, that is to say in the middle of a long, straight alleyway, lined with old fences and half tumbling walls, with a ruined pavilion as a landmark.

As I feared that I would not be able to find the place by myself, we decided to meet, for that excursion, in the same café where we had already stopped today. Their beer might be more palatable than their black coffee.

But the taxi driver was getting impatient; he claimed that his vehicle was holding up traffic, which was quite stupid, since there was no traffic at all. Yet, it was getting close to train time, so Simon and I said brief good-byes. At the last moment, he called out a phone number where I could reach him: seven sixty-five, forty-three, twenty-one.

Once settled into the cab, which was old and in even worse shape than the New York City cabs, I noticed that it was also that bright yellow color we are used to at home, but which is very unusual in France. Simon, however, was not surprised.

And still thinking about it some more, I began to wonder how that car had appeared precisely along our way: taxis are not accustomed to cruising such deserted places, practically uninhabited. That would be hard to understand. . . .

I became even more concerned when I realized the driver had placed his rearview mirror, atop the windshield, in such a way that he could easily observe me, instead of watching the street behind us. When I met his eyes, in the small rectangular mirror, he didn't even look away. He had strong, irregular, asymmetrical features. And I thought he looked sinister.

Disturbed by these dark, deep-set eyes, that remained fixed upon me in the mirror (was he then familiar with this maze of alleyways, that he could drive through them this way at a good speed almost without looking at the road?), I asked if the Gare du Nord were still far away. The man then twisted his mouth horribly, in what was perhaps a failed attempt at a smile, and said, in a slow voice:

"Don't you worry, we'll be there soon enough."

That innocuous reply, spoken in a mournful tone (someone prone to panic might even have found it threatening), only increased my concern. Then, I blamed myself for my excessive mistrust, and thought that Simon's wild imagination was probably contagious.

I had thought I was very close to the station, when we had parted, Simon and I. However, the cab drove on for a long time, through neighborhoods where nothing was familiar, and which looked to me more like distant suburbs.

Then, suddenly, at a turn in the street, we found ourselves in front of the well-known facade of the

Gare du Nord. At the edge of the sidewalk, at a place where cabs unload their passengers after a quick U-turn, there was Simon waiting for me.

He opened the door for me politely, and he must have paid the fare himself, because, after I saw him lean briefly into the driver's open window, the cab sped away, full speed, without waiting for anything else. However, that exchange of words (inaudible) had been extremely short, and I do not recall having seen, between the two men, the slightest gesture in any way related to some transaction.

I was, besides, absolutely flabbergasted by this unexpected reappearance of Simon. He smiled sweetly, looking happy, like a child who has played a good trick. I asked him how he had got there.

"Ah well," he said to me, "I took a shortcut."

"You walked?"

"Of course. And I've been waiting for you for ten minutes already."

"But that's impossible!"

"It may be impossible, but it's true. You took a very long time to drive that short distance. Now, you have missed your train, and your friend."

It was unfortunately true. I was almost ten minutes late, and I was going to have a hard time finding Caroline in the crowd. I was supposed to be waiting for her as she got off the train, just at the gate exit from the platform.

"If you want my opinion," Simon added moreover, "that driver took you the long way around on purpose, just to make it a bigger fare. Since you took so long to get here, I even thought for a moment that you'd never arrive: yellow cabs are always the ones used in kidnappings. It's a tradition in this country.

"You'll have to be more suspicious from now on: more than a dozen pretty girls, in just this way, disappear every day in Paris. They'll spend the remainder of their short lives in the luxurious brothels of Beirut, Macao, or Buenos Aires. Just last month they discovered . . ."

Then suddenly, as though he had in a flash remembered some urgent business, Simon broke off, in the midst of his fabrications and lies, and declared hurriedly:

"Excuse me, I must be gone. I have lingered here too long. Till tomorrow, then, as agreed."

He had spoken, to remind me of our meeting the next day, in a low and mysterious voice, like one who might have feared the indiscreet ears of possible spies. I answered: "See you tomorrow!" and I saw him watched him hurry away. He was soon lost in the crowd.

I then turned back toward the entrance of the station, and I saw Caroline coming out, walking toward me with her broadest smile. To my great surprise, she was holding by the hand a little blond girl, very pretty, maybe seven or eight years old.

Caroline, whose right hand was encumbered with a suitcase, let go of the little girl's hand to wave at me cheerfully with her left. And she called out to me,

unconcerned about the travelers hurrying in all di-
rections between her and me:

"So, that's the way you wait for me on the platform! You just stand there, talking with guys, without caring about when my train comes in!"

She ran up to me and kissed me with her usual
exuberance. The little girl looked the other way, with
the discreet air of a well-bred young lady who hasn't
been introduced yet. I said:

"Yes, I know, I am a bit late. Forgive me. I'll explain to you . . ."

"There's nothing to explain: I saw you with that
good-looking guy! Here, this is Marie. She's the
daughter of my brother Joseph and of Jeanne. She
was entrusted to me in Amsterdam, to bring her back
to her parents."

The child then performed for my benefit, with
earnestness, a complicated and ceremonious curtsey,
such as young ladies were taught fifty or a hundred
years ago. I said: "Hello, Marie!" and Caroline continued her explanations with animation:

"She was spending her vacation at an aunt's, you
know: Jeanne's sister who married an officer in the
Russian Navy. I already told you the story: a man
named Boris, who asked for political asylum when
his ship made port in The Hague."

Speaking in the reasonable tone of a grown-up,
and in surprisingly sophisticated language for a child
her age, little Marie added her own commentary:

"Uncle Boris is not really a political refugee. He's

a Soviet agent, disguised as a dissident, whose mission is to spread discontent and disorder among workers in the nuclear industry.

"And you found that out all by yourself?" I asked her with amusement.

"Yes, I did," she answered, unperturbed. "I did see that he had his spy number tattooed in blue on his left wrist. He tries to hide it under a leather wristband, which he wears supposedly to strengthen that joint. But that can't be true, since he does no physical work."

"Don't pay any attention to Marie," Caroline told me. "She's always inventing absurd stories of science fiction, espionage, or the occult. Children read far too much fantastic literature."

At that moment, I realized that a man was watching us, a few steps away from us. He stood a little way back, in an angle of the wall, and stared at our little group with abnormal interest. At first, I thought it was Marie who was attracting his rather unwholesome interest.

He might have been about forty, perhaps a little more, and he wore a gray, doublebreasted suit of classic cut (with matching jacket, vest and pants), but it was old, threadbare, shapeless with wear, and his shirt and tie were as beat up as though he had slept in his clothes during some very long train trip. He carried in his hand a small, black leather case, which made me think of a surgeon's kit, I don't exactly know why.

Those dark and piercing eyes, deeply set, that face with its heavy, asymmetrical, sharply etched, unpleasant features, that wide mouth twisted into a kind of smirk, all that reminded me brutally of something . . . a memory, however recent, that I could not manage to bring into focus.

Then, suddenly, I remembered: it was the driver of the yellow cab who had brought me to the station. I experienced such a sharp sense of discomfort, almost physical, that I felt myself blushing. I turned my head away from that unpleasant character. But a few seconds later, I glanced at him again.

He had neither moved, nor changed the direction of his stare. But it was rather Caroline, to tell the truth, whom he seemed to be watching. Did I forget to mention that Caroline is a very beautiful girl? Tall, a great body, slender, very blond, with a short haircut and a sweet, slightly androgynous face, one that brings to mind that of the actress Jane Frank, she always attracts the homage, more or less indiscreet, of men of all ages.

I must also confess something else: people claim that there is an extraordinary resemblance between us. We are generally mistaken for two sisters, often even for twins. And it has happened several times that friends of Caroline addressed me, thinking they were speaking to her, which one day triggered a strange adventure. . . .

But Caroline interrupted the course of my thoughts:

"What's the matter with you?" she asked, scrutinizing my face with concern. "Your expression has changed. You look like you've just seen something scary."

Marie, who had guessed the cause of my emotion, explained calmly, in a loud voice:

"The guy who's been following us since we got off the train is still here, with his little suitcase full of knives. He's a (sex) pervert, obviously, I could tell right away."

"Don't talk so loud," whispered Caroline, bending over the child while pretending to smooth the rumpled folds of her dress, "he's going to hear us."

"Of course he can hear us," answered Marie without lowering her voice. "That's what he's here for."

And, suddenly, she stuck out her tongue at the stranger, and at the same time smiled her most angelic smile at him. Caroline burst out laughing, with her customary unconcern, while scolding Marie as a matter of principle, without any conviction. Then she said to me:

"In fact, the child might be right. Besides, I think that character took the same train we were on. It seems to me that I saw him prowling in the corridor, and that I had already spotted him on the departure platform, in Amsterdam."

Raising my eyes once more toward the suspicious character with the black case, I then witnessed a scene that only served to increase my astonishment.

117

The man was no longer turned toward us; he was now looking at a blind man who walked toward him, feeling the ground with the iron tip of his cane.

He was a tall, blond young man, twenty or twenty-five, wearing an elegant windbreaker made of very fine leather, cream colored, and open over a bright blue pullover. Black goggles hid his eyes. He held in his right hand a white cane with a curved handle. A little boy of about twelve was leading him by the left hand.

For a few seconds, I imagined, against all likelihood, that it was Simon Lecoeur, who was returning disguised as a blind man. Of course, looking at him more carefully, I soon recognized my error: the few points of resemblance that one could find in the general appearance, the dress, or the hairstyle of the two men, were in fact minor.

When the young man with the white cane and his guide got close to the character with the baggy clothes and the physician's bag, they stopped. But none of them gave any sign whatever. There were no salutations, none of those words or gestures of welcome that might have been expected in such circumstances. They remained there without saying a word, face to face, motionless now.

Then, with deliberate precision, in the same even motion, precisely as if the same mechanism were activating three heads, they turned toward us. And they remained that way, petrified once again, motionless now like three statues: the young man with the fair face half-hidden behind his bulky glasses, framed between the little boy on his left and the short man in the shapeless gray suit on his right.

All three kept their eyes fixed on me, the blind man too, I could have sworn it, behind his enormous black lenses. The skinny face of the boy had an extreme, abnormal, ghostly pallor. The ugly features of the short man had frozen into a horrible grimace. The whole group suddenly seemed to me so terrifying that I wanted to scream, as one does to end a nightmare.

But, just as in nightmares, no sound came out of my mouth. Why wasn't Caroline saying anything? And what about Marie, who was standing between the two of us, why wasn't she breaking the spell, bold and casual as children will be? Why was she standing there frozen, rendered speechless too, held in thrall by what enchantment?

Anguish was growing in me so dangerously, relentless, that I feared I might faint. To struggle against this unbearable malaise, so unlike my nature, I tried to think of something else. But I could no longer find anything to hold on to, except one of the idiotic tirades Simon was delivering for my benefit an hour or two earlier:

I was not, he claimed, a real woman, but only a highly sophisticated electronic robot built by a certain Dr. Morgan. Dr. Morgan was now subjecting me to various experiments in order to test my performance. He was putting me through a series of tests, while having me watched by agents in his employ, placed everywhere along my way, some of whom, themselves, would be nothing but robots as well. . . .

The gestures of that phony blind man, who had just arrived as though by chance in front of me, did they not, precisely, seem to me mechanical and staccato? Those strange goggles, which seemed to be growing monstrously larger, were probably not covering real eyes, but a sophisticated recording system, perhaps even some device that emitted rays, which were working, unbeknownst to me, on my body and on my consciousness. And the surgeon-cabdriver was none other than Morgan himself.

The space between these people and me had emptied, I know not through what chance circumstance, or what supernatural action. The travelers milling around here in large numbers a moment earlier, had disappeared now. . . . With incomprehensible difficulty, I managed to turn my head away from those three pairs of eyes that hypnotized me. And I sought help in the direction of Marie and Caroline.

They too were staring at me with the same icy, inhuman eyes. They were not on my side, but on that of the others, against me. . . . I felt my legs giving way, and my reason tumbling, into the void, in a vertiginous fall.

When I woke up this morning, my head was empty, heavy, and my mouth felt pasty, as though I had allowed myself, the day before, to drink to excess, or else taken some powerful sleeping drug. Yet that was not the case.

What did I do, exactly, the night before? I could not manage to remember. . . . I was supposed to go and meet Caroline at the station, but something prevented me. . . . I no longer knew what it was.

A picture, however, came back to my memory, but I couldn't tie it to anything. It was a large room, furnished with odd pieces, in very bad repair, like those sprung chairs and those broken iron bedsteads that used to be relegated to the attics of old houses.

There were, in particular, a very large number of old trunks, of different sizes and shapes. I opened one. It was full of old-fashioned women's clothing, corsets, petticoats, pretty faded dresses of another day. I could not very well make out the elaborate ornaments or the embroidery, because the room was lit by only two candelabra in which candle stubs burned with a yellow and vacillating flame. . . .

Next, I thought of the ad that Caroline had read me, over the phone, when she called to tell me the arrival time of her train. Since I was looking for a part-time job, in order to supplement the amount of my scholarship, I had decided to go to the address given in that weird job ad, which my friend had found while reading an ecological weekly. But I had overslept so long, today, that the time to get ready had already come, if I wanted to be there at the appointed hour.

I arrived exactly at six-thirty. It was almost dark

already. The hangar wasn't locked. I walked in by pushing the door, which no longer had a lock.

Inside, all was silent. Under the faint light that came through the windows with dirt-encrusted panes, I could barely see the objects that surrounded me, piled everywhere in great disarray, probably cast off.

When my eyes became used to the semidarkness, I finally noticed the man facing me. Standing, motionless, both hands in the pockets of his raincoat, he watched me without speaking a word, without so much as the slightest greeting in my direction.

Resolutely, I stepped forward toward him. . . .

EPILOGUE

Here stops Simon Lecoeur's story.
I do say "Simon Lecoeur's story" because no one—neither our people, nor those on the side of the police—thinks that Chapter Eight, supposedly written by a woman, was really written by anyone else: it is too clearly integrated into the whole, from the grammatical point of view as well as according to the logic of the plot locales and the narrative twists.

Simon—all testimony agrees on this point—came

as usual to teach his class, at the school on the rue de Passy, on Thursday May eighth early in the afternoon. "He looked worried," several of his students stated at the time of the inquest. But most of them added that he always looked worried.

He displayed, in fact, a disturbing combination of almost pathological nervousness, incompletely restrained anxiety, and a sweet, smiling lightness that had a great deal to do with the definite charisma that everyone agreed he possessed. In the most casual hallway conversation with a colleague, a student, or even a superior, he offered such easy chatty friendliness, full of casual and unexpected inventiveness, spontaneity, inconsequential humor, that he was liked by everyone, as one loves a child. . . .

Then, suddenly, the innocent smile would vanish from his lips, which would lose in a few seconds their attractive, sensuous lines to become hard and thin; his eyes seemed to sink deeper, his pupils darkened. . . . And he would turn around abruptly, as though he would thus come face to face with an enemy who had approached him behind his back, silently. . . . But there was no one, and Simon would slowly resume his previous demeanor, before his bewildered interlocutor. Bewildered himself, the young man seemed then to have fled thousands of miles, or even light years away. He would then take leave on a few vague, incoherent, barely audible words.

On Friday, May ninth, he did not show up at school. That caused no concern: his Friday class,

124

scheduled at the end of the day, was the last of the week, and many students—especially in the spring—made it a point to consider attendance optional: it sometimes happened that young instructors did the same.

But on Monday the twelfth, he was not seen again either, nor on Tuesday. His room did not have a phone. On Wednesday, an assistant director asked the students whether one of them could stop by the rue d'Amsterdam in order to enquire about the health of "Ján," who might have been seriously ill and unable to notify anyone. The volunteer messenger said she found a closed door. There was no answer to her repeated rings or her calls. No sound came from within.

Thursday the fifteenth was Ascension Day. On Friday the sixteenth in the morning, school authorities alerted the police. Simon Lecoeur's door was broken in, in the presence of a police commissioner, that Friday around noon.

In the room as in the bathroom, the inspectors found everything in order, just as our agents (they, obviously, possessed a duplicate key) already had two days earlier. There was no evidence of a struggle, or of any untimely visit, or hurried departure. The ninety-nine typed pages (which we had been careful to replace after Xeroxing) soon became therefore the only element that could be considered a clue.

The interest of the investigators in that text only grew, as one can guess, when, on Sunday the eighteenth, around seven P.M., there was discovered in an abandoned workshop, near the Gare du Nord, the lifeless body of an unknown woman, about twenty years old. She hadn't been dead for more than an hour, perhaps even less.

The young victim was carrying no document that might help to identify her. But her physical appearance, her clothing, her exact position on the ground (as well as the location itself, besides) were exactly as described in Chapter Six of Simon's story. As he had indicated, the puddle of blood was not real blood. The coroner noted right away that the body showed no injury, no external trauma, the causes of death remaining therefore undiscovered. It appeared nevertheless almost beyond doubt that it was a case of murder, and not of natural death.

All investigations concerning the identity of the young woman have, so far, yielded no clues: no person answering her description has been reported missing anywhere in the country. Because of the proximity of the railroad station, investigations are now being directed toward Antwerp or Amsterdam.

Another point puzzles the police; the more than curious resemblance (general appearance, measurements, facial features, color of the eyes and the hair, etc.) that exists between the dead girl and Simon Lecoeur himself. The matter is so disturbing that it was believed for a while that they were one and the same person: the charming professor of the Franco-American School would have been a female transvestite. This attractive hypothesis was not however retained, for the school physician had given the so-called Simon a thorough physical some two weeks earlier, and he guaranteed that Simon did belong to the masculine sex.

That practitioner—Dr. Morgan—was treating Simon for eye problems, acute troubles, it seems, although they were probably of nervous origin. The missing man claimed, indeed, to have been experiencing with increased frequency sudden moments of diminished vision (decreased luminosity of the images on the retina), sometimes to the point of total blindness, lasting occasionally for several long minutes. Morgan, given to psychoanalysis, had immediately thought of an everyday Oedipus complex.

The patient had only laughed off the suggestion, saying he had nothing to do at Cologne. That absurd pun, linked to the theme of the disjointed paving stones, continued to plunge the physician into deep perplexity, and renewed his suspicions. It cannot be ruled out, of course, that our sometime blind man was an ordinary faker, but his motives aren't clear, since he wasn't asking his employer for any sick leave, nor the slightest change of schedule.

Of all the characters that appear in his story, one in any case—at least—does exist without any doubt: little Marie. Starting from the abandoned workshop, investigators had no trouble finding the café where they don't serve pizza. A policeman watched the establishment for several days. Little Marie, still in her

1880-style dress, walked in on the evening of the twenty-first (she was coming, as it will be learned later, to pay off an old debt). As she was leaving, the policeman tailed her. He followed her to the Ver-cingétorix dead end. About halfway down the long alleyway, some of our people stepped in. Having quietly intercepted that overzealous guardian of law and order, they brought him back, once more, to square one.